THE LEGACY

OF

UNCLE JULES

♦ a young adult mystery ♦

by

Roberta Georgiou

THE LEGACY OF UNCLE JULES
Novel © 2013 by Roberta Georgiou
ISBN: 978-0-9889350-2-0

The characters and events in this book are fictional.
Any resemblance to real people or situations
is entirely coincidental.

ACKNOWLEDGEMENTS

Thank you, Louise, for inspiring this story and thank you ever so much, Sarah, for your technical help.

I also extend deep gratitude to friends, family, and colleagues who supported me in this literary journey. Special thanks go to Ken Cheney, whose insight helped shape the writing and taught me how to reread with ever-so-imperative fresh eyes.

CHAPTER 1

Chrys counted to sixty as she pumped the pedals of her bike. At least sixty more days to be with him. Sixty more talks to add to her mental scrapbook. Sixty more opportunities to say "I love you."

Borrowed time, he had told her, should never be wasted.

Having left school as soon as the last bell rang on this last day of her sophomore year, Chrys pedaled furiously over the remaining three miles to Uncle Jules and Aunt Lydia's house. On a straight, downhill stretch of road, she let go of the handlebars and flung open her arms as though she could lift off like a kite. She was free, free, free for the entire summer to visit her uncle, who understood her better than anyone—sometimes better than herself.

She pictured him smiling at her with his pearly white teeth and the flashes of gold crowns at the sides, and his arms outstretched like the boughs of a great tree. The ritual was always the same. He first gave her a bear hug and then tweaked her cheek.

Just yesterday he had done that and again told her, "You're a strong girl, and strong girls do heroic things."

"I'm going to be great…." she mused.

"Chrys, people are people. But some have the toughness to accomplish important things." He put his hand on her arm. "But you must also keep your brothers and sister close together in 'these strange times.' And you're just the one

1

who can do that."

"How do you know my future?"

"I can feel it. Didn't I tell you about the time I went to Lilydale?"

"You did? Really?" Chrys squealed. "The town of spiritualists?"

"I did. What a revelation…"

"Did you get a reading?"

He looked at his watch. "It'll have to wait. It's suppertime at your house. And I'm afraid you're already late."

"Oh, I don't care about eating." She made a face of disgust. "Tonight's pot roast."

"Oooh that horrible, Gothic monster of a dish!" he said, wincing. "Quoth the raven: Nevermore!"

Both of them laughed.

He cleared his throat. "Let's keep this between you, me, and Edgar Allan Poe, okay? We wouldn't want to offend your mother."

"She won't care if I'm not there for dinner. So what about Lilydale?"

"Chrys … You and I both know if you don't show up for a meal she's cooked, it'll hurt her feelings. Look, I promise to tell you every little eerie detail tomorrow. Unless, of course, you'd rather spend the time driving some boy 'to despair, near madness or death.' He winked at her. "How many is it now?"

"Oh stop!" she said, trying not to smile. She got up, leaned over, and gave him a kiss on the cheek. "Okay, I'll be here right after school."

If her father had kidded her that way, she would have rolled her eyes, turned up her nose, said, "Honestly, Dad, I'm not a child," and stomped away. But it was different with Uncle Jules. Maybe the reason was simply that he wasn't her

2

father. Maybe it had to do with his being a high school English teacher. No, he was just a genuine kid-whisperer.

Unlike her father, a Certified Public Accountant who took himself and everything seriously, Uncle Jules never took himself seriously and never expected anyone else to either. But that's exactly why Chrys and her siblings did. Plus, he had a special way with each of them and had given them a host of memories: his corny gifts, the Shakespearian quotations for every occasion, the creative explanations he offered for why things happened or didn't—like why lightning bugs didn't stay lit—not to mention the scary stories he told while they huddled around the fire by their lake.

As soon as Chrys turned onto Uncle Jules' street, her heart thumped. Her parents' cars were parked in the driveway, and it was only one o'clock. She could barely catch her breath as she pedaled on and screeched to a stop in front of the house. She jumped off, dropped her bike to the ground, and bolted to the front door. She swung it wide and rushed in, but halfway through the house, her mother intercepted her. Chrys tried to walk on toward her uncle's bedroom, but her mother wrapped her arms tightly around her.

Her voice breaking, she said, "He's not there, Chrys."

"What happened? He had two months, maybe three."

"I know, but all a doctor can do is guess. The rest is up to the patient and—"

"Then I don't understand," Chrys said defiantly. "Love is stronger than anything. And he loved Aunt Lydia and us more than anything. And we loved him." She was silent for some moments then asked, "When...?"

"Eleven fifteen."

Her mother tried to say more but the words seemed unable to move past her vocal chords. Then when she did manage to say her twin brother's given name—Julius—a great spasm seized her and she burst into tears. She took Chrys by the arm and led her to the living room couch, where they sat on the edge next to each other. Her mother pulled a tissue from her sweater pocket and sobbed into it. Chrys hugged her from the side but said nothing, knowing no words that could help either of them. Instead, she slowly rubbed her mother's back. Chrys looked at the clock on the mantel and thought about what she had been doing two hours earlier. Throughout her last exam she had felt nothing odd. She thoroughly believed in extra sensory perception and so every day she waited for her powers to materialize. Especially in this case, why hadn't she sensed the change in her uncle's condition?

Finally, as a squall erupts and just as quickly subsides, so did her mother's tears and shudders of sadness. She sat back and studied Chrys with concern.

"Honey, it's okay to cry."

"I ... I just can't believe it. Losing him seems so sudden."

"But you knew that anything could happen. Like today when his heart stopped...."

Chrys mused, "So he died of a broken heart. And now you have one." She drew a quick breath. "Oh, and Aunt Lydia. Her heart must be in a billion pieces."

Her mother's eyes welled up with tears and she gently patted Chrys's shoulder, but Chrys shrugged it away, slipped to the floor and crossed her legs. Staring at the area rug and twisting a loose thread, she said. "I should have been here." She looked up at her mother. "You should have come and gotten me."

"Oh no, Sweetie. It was much better that you were in school today. You know he would have wanted it that way."

"But it may have helped."

4

Her mother looked astonished. "Nothing could have prolonged his life."

Chrys hung her head. Her mother hadn't understood. "I know," she said softly. "I just wanted to be here, that's all."

Chrys glanced up to see her mother peering at her as though Chrys had grown a third eye.

"You saw how much weight your uncle lost over these last three weeks." She sniffled and dabbed the corner of her eyes with the tissue.

Chrys couldn't begin to set her mother straight when her mother's mind was obviously wobbling in and out of reason like that of a badly beaten boxer. Chrys wanted to be by her uncle's side not because she felt she could have cast a spell and saved him and not because she had developed some morbid curiosity about death. She should have been there to help her mind and heart understand. To help her shake the overwhelming feeling that he really wasn't dead.

Her mother broke into sobs again but quickly suppressed them and hugged her. After gazing worriedly at Chrys's face—especially at the smooth space between Chrys's eyes where she had apparently grown that extra eye—her mother got up and left the room.

Chrys lay back on the rug and stared at the ceiling. Uncle Jules' face immediately appeared to her and she could hear his voice laughing and joking as though he were right in front of her. She tried over and over again to erase it but try as she might, she couldn't picture her precious uncle, the most alive person she had ever met, lifeless.

Over the next two days Chrys's house teemed with activity. The change in everyone's behavior seemed perfectly reasonable for people who accepted his death: the chaotic actions of her mother, the quiet meditation of her father, the unusual politeness between her brothers, the raspier breathing of her asthmatic sister and the haunting vacancy in Aunt Lydia's eyes. Still, Chrys felt distant from the others as if she were a scientific observer of grief. Often she expected Uncles Jules to walk through the door as blithe as you please and check on her note-taking skills.

The day before the funeral as she watched her mother's nonstop action, Chrys was reminded of a poem her uncle had taught each year over his eighteen-year career—written by Emily Dickinson. Or just "Emily" as he called her. (He said his ability to recite hundreds of her poems gave him the right to be on a first-name basis with her.) The poem was entitled "The Bustle in a House" and spoke of the countless things to take care of after a death. Then when the commotion is over, the time comes for "sweeping up the heart and putting love away."

With the confusion of meal times in the last two days and her parents' sporadic comings and goings, as well as the visits of neighbors, friends, and relatives, Chrys understood the "bustle in her house." But she wondered whether after the funeral, the final turmoil, her mother would be able to pack up and put away her love for her only sibling. Could any of them? Especially Aunt Lydia. Because according to "Emily" and Uncle Jules, you can't live and be sane if you don't.

CHAPTER 2

It should have been raining. Drizzling at the very least. Standing at her uncle's grave, Chrys looked at the cloudless sky, blue as a robin's egg, and wished that a rogue cloud would gallop up, drench the scene and stream some of its tears down her face. This was a funeral after all, and deserved proper weather. In literature it did, her uncle would say.

Seeing that all the people around her were mopping up tears, she now worried that they would notice her dry eyes. She would love her uncle until the end of time, and tears were the surest sign of sincerity. So why couldn't she cry?

A drone then started up. The low and dirge-like sound of the minister's voice would surely make her weep. But at his first pause another sound mixed in. A couple of songbirds in two different trees twittered at each other. God-Quest must have mis-mapped them from the cheery wedding where they were supposed to be.

Her mother, who was standing at her right side and whose chest had been heaving with silent wails, suddenly became as still as a blade of grass. The minister finished his last sentence and the "Amen" just before the casket settled into the grave. And so the moment had come for Aunt Lydia to cast the first shovel of earth and bury him forever.

Chrys looked into the open grave and now knew why she couldn't cry. It wasn't because she didn't miss him but because he wasn't gone. She knew it as surely as she now realized why it wasn't raining. Whatever lay in that casket wasn't Uncle Jules. She wished she could have shared this revelation with her mother, who now looked as though she needed a stretcher to make it to the car, but a backlight in Chrys's brain, like a roadside beacon, warned her to keep silent.

She glanced at her two brothers and her sister. Peri, a year younger, wasn't openly crying but blinking madly just the same. Twelve-year-old William continued to blubber as he'd done since they left the church. Iris, William's twin, stared at the casket with tear-tracks down her face and though she breathed laboriously, she looked catatonic all the same. Only their father seemed to be taking the whole scene calmly. Still, he had a sad look on his face. Chrys assumed he was merely being strong for them. Otherwise, she felt certain he would have been weeping too. Too often he had belly-laughed with Uncle Jules not to love him like a brother. In the last few weeks, Chrys had a couple times caught her father glossy-eyed enough to rub his face or look away and clear his throat. Chrys ran her hands over her face, hoping….

They spent the next three hours at Aunt Lydia's where everyone ate and reminisced. Chrys spent most of the time alone by the lake in the back.

On the drive home she noticed the family's eyes on her. One by one her siblings looked at her in disbelief, sometimes, it seemed, with resentment. Once, her mother turned around and asked her if she was all right, and when she answered "yes," she caught her father's eyes peering at her from the rearview mirror. What should she do? Should she pinch that tissue between her nostrils to bring tears to her eyes? Should she fix her thoughts on that last sad movie she'd watched? But if the way Uncle Jules looked the last time she saw him and watching his coffin being scattered with dirt couldn't make her eyes burn, then what would?

Finally, their car pulled into the driveway. Thank goodness. Chrys could now fling open the car door then dash to the house and up to her room. With such an action no one would suspect that she wasn't finally overcome with a cascade of tears.

Her plan went just as she imagined. But to play out the scene and make it believable, she felt she had to pass the rest of that evening alone in her room. She heard little stirring from the floor below. No movies blaring. No feet pounding on the stairs and angry remarks volleying between Peri and William. Only the occasional muffled voices of her parents from the den beneath her room.

Chrys flopped across her bed. Lazily, she flipped through the new issue of *Victoria's Secret* that each month her mother made sure ended up in Chrys's room, but Chrys had never been tempted to go beyond the near-naked body on the front cover. Still, she was eager to keep her mind occupied. After turning only a few pages, Chrys realized *Land's End* was more her style. As she tossed the catalog to the floor, her door slowly swung open. Her mother stepped in as though unsure there was a floor to support her.

She handed Chrys a package. "It must be the book you ordered." She turned to the door but before leaving asked again, "Are you going to be okay?"

Even though Chrys heard Uncle Jules' velvet voice resounding in her mother's, she simply nodded.

"All right then. But if you need to talk…."

Chrys nodded again.

After her mother closed the door behind her, Chrys opened the package and flipped through the book, *Channeling Dead Spirits*. She was anxious to read about mediumship to discover how Uncle Jules' trip to Lilydale might have enlightened him. But a mere five minutes later she heard her mother from downstairs break into such violent and continuous sobs that she couldn't read on, so she exchanged the book for what would transport her from reality—music. She got up, sat at her desk and slipped on the headset. Song after song streamed into her brain while she sketched a dark blue evening studded with fireflies and a campfire by her uncle's lake. Hours later she slipped off the headphones. For the first time in her life, she was aware of the solitude that a house, and more importantly, her room could afford. Surely there were moments like these in the past, but she couldn't recall a time when utter silence echoed in her ears.

She got up, opened her door and gazed up and down the hall. From the darkness and the quiet, she guessed that all the others were asleep. With a passion she wished she were a bear with a full belly in December. She glared at the clock with insomniac eyes, and the clock glared its greenish three o'clock eyes back at her. The problem wasn't that she had to get up early like her parents. She just wished this day would end. She crawled into bed, hoping the warmth would relax her body into sleepiness. She stretched her arms up and feet down as far as she could. She folded her arms behind her head and closed her eyes.

Without relief all the day's images kept swirling in front of her like an ever-changing kaleidoscope. If she were ever to nod off, they had to stop. So she rolled onto her side, thinking that turning her head would change her mental channel. She yawned deeply. Finally feeling as worn out as an old rag, she felt that she could actually drift off. She pulled up the covers over her shoulder and burrowed her face into the pillow.

Within seconds a strange but soft light penetrated her eyelids. It gradually grew brighter as if on a dimmer switch. She knew it was not the glow of the clock on the nightstand or the beam of a flashlight that Peri had once used to scare her out of her skin in the middle of the night. Or even the faint hint of the moon. Rather, the light seemed to penetrate the pillow and was bluish like smoke. She rolled over and sat up on her elbows. She opened her eyes wide and blinked several times to make sure she wasn't dreaming.

Uncle Jules, who everyone (everyone but her, of course) had felt was buried that same day at five o'clock stood like a statue at the foot of her bed. A blue haze outlined his entire body and seemed to expand his dimensions. She stared at him, unable to tell where her uncle ended and the light began. Even though she could see every detail about him—right down to the Shakespearian quote on his shirt that read, "Doubt truth to be a liar; But never doubt I love"—she could also see through him to the pictures hanging on the far wall. They shifted slightly to the right, startling Chrys. But it wasn't the pictures that had moved. Uncle Jules had.

She shot back against the headboard and a squeak popped out of her. Uncle Jules leaned forward, stretched out his arms to her and smiled.

"Chrys, please don't be afraid," he said. With every word, golden rays of light shot from his lips.

She put her trembling hand to her mouth. "Uncle Jules?"

"Yes, Big Flower, it's me."

She smiled. He was the only one who referred to her that way, a left-handed compliment, of course, like calling her Big Cheese in a lovable way. This time, though, she couldn't muster a laugh or pretend to be insulted. She was worried for him.

"Uncle Jules, you're a ... a ... ghost." She didn't know whether she should have said that, but she was afraid he didn't know he was dead. Was that why he was in her room? Was she supposed to help him cross over? After all, she did have all the rules of the "after-road." She had read every documented ghost story and book about the paranormal she could get her hands on. She now fretted that she hadn't read more of her new book.

Uncle Jules seemed rooted to that spot at the end of her bed, yet he grew closer. "I know I'm a spirit," he said. "We'll use that word, all right? 'Ghost' is so ... so ... ghastly."

"Too Poe-like?" she asked.

"Oh, not for me;" he said and then in a low voice added, " it's mostly the science teachers and CPAs who object." He put his hands on his hips and chuckled. Chrys smiled at the light-hearted jab at her father. Suddenly, Uncle Jules glanced away then nodded as though answering someone not in the room. Looking back at her, he said, "Look, Chrys, I was granted a wish to return to my old life for a very important reason."

"Then why did you leave us in the first place?"

"I didn't leave," he said sweetly. "I wasn't permitted to stay."

She sat up straight, leaned forward and grabbed the comforter in her fists. "And so you're here on a mission?" she whispered.

"Yes, if you will, a mission. But one I can't perform on my own."

"To get you out of limbo?"

"No, no, I'm fine," he said. "It's a 'mission' to benefit the living."

"Oh," she said, disappointed that her expert knowledge was going to be wasted. But overlapping that feeling was her sense of loyalty and curiosity, which was growing as fast as a flame down a match. "What is it you want me to do?"

He knelt down and rested his forearms on the end of her bed. He seemed to take on warmer, earthier colors. His eyes appeared almost as mellow brown as she remembered with flecks of sunlight in them. Her shoulders relaxed and she took her first loose breath.

"There's a treasure," he said and his eyes twinkled, "very valuable, for someone in need. I thought you could help me get it to them. Of all four children, you are the bravest. And I'm afraid this won't be easy ... in many ways."

Chrys beamed. "Tell me what to do."

"Then listen very carefully." He looked upward rather than at the clock. "I don't have much time." And he clipped off the words as quickly but as clearly as he could. "Between two houses that aren't houses, that's where you'll find it." Then he stood very tall and his whole body glimmered for a few seconds like heat lightning.

"Oh please don't go!" Chrys panicked at seeing him disintegrate further. "What does that mean? How am I supposed to find the treasure with just that?"

Very deliberately he said, "It's between two houses of great sadness."

"What is? And what should I do with the treasure when I find it? Who does it belong to?"

"It's all there. All your answers are there. In the higher dwelling of the two, but you must step very carefully." He flickered again more intensely.

"Wait! Wait! What happened at Lilydale?"

He blew her a kiss. "Chrys, you don't need Lilydale…."

She was agonized with more questions and especially with a proper farewell. In all the books she had read about the spirit world, she knew how important closure—saying farewell but not goodbye—was for both the living and the dying. Still, instead of speaking, she clutched his kiss mid-air, slipped it under her pillow, and blew him a kiss in return. As in the past he caught her kiss in his hand, put it into his shirt pocket, and patted it close to his heart. She now understood they had performed the fondest of farewells—communicated in perfect wordlessness.

The warm tones of his eyes, skin, and hair faded completely. She lurched forward on the bed and reached to him. But every part of him transformed into sparkly nuggets. In another blink they vanished.

She flopped back on her pillow. Mixed emotions churned in her heart. She loved Uncle Jules almost as much as she loved her parents, and she was bursting with gladness over his visit. On the other hand, she absolutely hated riddles. And Uncle Jules knew it. So this was another of his jokes played on her, she wondered, like the time he told her to think of anything but pink elephants, and that was all she could think of the rest of the day. But this time she couldn't tease him back with a joke of her own. The worst of it, though, was that now she'd never go to sleep. She looked at the clock now screaming three-twenty and lay down on her back with her arms once again folded under her head.

"Houses that aren't houses," she repeated. And she tried to think of all the words she knew that had "house" in them. As though counting sheep she mumbled, "Houseboat ... doghouse ... birdhouse ... light house ... but there were no light houses in Ohio.... jailhouse ... but Uncle Jules would never have considered sending her there. She then remembered and said aloud, "To benefit the living," and with the weight of those words, she suddenly, miraculously knew where to go. Oh, but if her mother ever found out, Chrys thought as she pulled the covers up and snuggled in, she'd have a flame-throwing fit.

CHAPTER 3

The following morning Chrys clicked on the makeup mirror on her desk, pulled her chair up close and winced. Her eyes were so puffy and her face so drawn from the lack of sleep that for a second she wondered how she was going to look as an old woman of forty. But in light of her day's adventure, that thought raced away. She turned her face from side to side, examining it for new blemishes. Oh, why worry? No one could detect them mixed in with the constellation of freckles across her cheeks and nose. Other girls spent all their money on makeup and six-part skin care regimens. Not her. Still, she batted her eyes and wished her lashes weren't so blond. A foot away and they seemed to disappear altogether. She had always been okay with seeing "plain" in the mirror, but now with zits galore and her face looking as baggy as an old chair, she saw "grotesque" stare back at her. "Oh great," she said, "I'm right out of a Gothic horror story."

She finger-combed her long, wavy hair and roughly gathered it into a ponytail. As she strapped on her watch, it blinked the time in big numbers. "I know. I know," she whispered to it. "I'm hurrying!" She stuffed a couple dollars into her jeans' pocket and sped downstairs.

Even if she could have come alive earlier, she knew better than to go into Willow when she might run into her mother. Even at this later hour of eleven, her mother would question why she wasn't still asleep or with friends. And

Chrys didn't lie or skirt the truth well. So she had to maneuver her day around her mother's lunch hour from work.

As though a tornado were at her back, she pedaled her ten-speed over the back roads that led to the town of Loyal Oak. A town? Hamlet maybe, with a single traffic light, a mom-and-pop grocery store on one corner, a gas station on another, a Twistee Cream on the third and a "tavern" (not a "bar") across from it. Home was this farming community on the shirttail of a real town, but she didn't mind living in the middle of nowhere. It was actually the best of all possible places. Within the same hour, she could pick wild blackberries and shop at Old Navy.

Stopping at the light in Loyal Oak, she glanced at her watch then pedaled off harder. Her destination was another five miles, and she was operating on precious time. Chrys now rode on the dirt edge of Elmview Road, a busy two-lane highway with large estates on either side. The road had once been lined with towering elms. But that was long before she was born. Her mother said the elms had all died from some horrible disease and left both the road and the houses barren. Chrys thought of her uncle and the cancer that had taken him, leaving her and her family utterly barren. She pumped the pedals more furiously, as though doing so would drive away the image of Uncle Jules, gray and gaunt, as he looked in his last days. He had been a great presence in their lives, now gone forever like one of those elms. She noticed a tree stump and wished there was another way she could go. But Elmview was the only route that directly linked her house to Willow. Two miles beyond Loyal Oak, she finally turned onto a less traveled road and so came into Willow from the north.

When she arrived at the first commercial city block, she got off her bike and tethered it to the rack outside the

16

library. The great wooden portal beckoned her to come in, but instead she took a deep breath, locked her bike to the spindle and strode away.

She would walk the rest of the way across town so she could dodge into a shop if she saw her mother. She checked the time again. By now her mother should be a few blocks away having lunch at Ramona's Tea Room. Once, Chrys had asked her mother why she ate there every day, why she didn't sometimes bag her lunch. Her mother said she preferred a place with fresh flowers where she could enjoy with friends a cup of hot tea and a warm meal. Simple pleasures, she said, was all she wanted in life. Chrys couldn't have disagreed more. She would be somebody important someday. Uncle Jules had often spelled out that she had remarkable "g-e-n-e-s" (not to be confused with "j-e-a-n-s," he said) and even from his grave he had mentioned the mark of greatness within her.

As she walked along, she gazed into shop windows. In each case her reflection blended with the goods in the window. At a jewelry store her green eyes hovered above an emerald necklace; at a bank her blond hair appeared above a pot of fake gold coins; in a travel agency showcase for a Caribbean Cruise, her silver key chain hooked to her belt dangled above a treasure chest with a ring of silver skeleton keys hanging from the lock. Understanding how the supernatural worked, Chrys saw these signs as assurance that she was on the right track. At the third traffic light, she looked to the left down Mulberry Avenue, a side street that dead-ended at her destination. She stared at the two five-story, grim-looking concrete buildings connected at the third floor with a walkway. Her chest heaved with anticipation.

"Hey Chrysler!" a boy's voice rang out. Chrys groaned in swinging around. "Quit calling me that! You don't know jack, Jack!"

17

"Yeah, sure," said Chuck, the tallest and biggest dolt of the three gangling teenagers slouching on the opposite street corner. He laughed loudly. "You can't fool us. We know you were named for what happened sixteen years ago in the backseat of your old man's car."

Two elderly women, coming out of the card shop, looked askance at him, but he laughed raucously, and the others followed suit. All three were students at Willow High. Fellow students, perhaps, but absolute jerks. A few times, though, she had regarded Jack, the smartest of the Malignant Marauders, as having a flea's leg of gentlemanly potential. That is, only when he was separated from his cretin companions.

She thought about spewing back at them the real story behind her name and end once and for all the upper hand they believed they had over her. But unfortunately, Jack had led the group to the sports store on the far corner of the intersection. Turning again toward her destination, she thought about her name and the problem it had caused her with those boys. Even if she had explained it to them, she knew the truth would probably have given them even more fuel for their lame teasing.

Total grayness suddenly surrounded her. She looked up from the sidewalk. Without realizing it, she had walked to the end of the side street. In front of her loomed the two buildings that she felt certain would supply the solution to Uncle Jules' riddle. His voice echoed in her mind, "Two houses that aren't houses ... a place of great sorrow." Well, if those twin buildings in front of her didn't fit that description, she didn't know what would. She started toward the front steps of the main building wondering excitedly what she would find and who the owner of the treasure would be. Still, she hesitated before the door, took a nervous step backward, and stared at the name engraved on the brass plate above the threshold: New Life Habitat.

CHAPTER 4

Chrys had never stood that close to those buildings before. Seeing some big patches of mildew on the walls, she thought they could use a good cleaning, one as good as its residents had gotten, both inside and out. A halfway house, this place was where reformed drug addicts lived and tried to find a productive life within the community. New Life Habitat was a fresh start for the down and out. It was also her mother's place of work.

Her mother, a psychologist who worked as a group therapist, often shared poignant stories with Chrys of the residents' struggle to stay clean, their joys when they did—and if they were still young—their reunions and re-bonding with their families. What her mother didn't share was her physical workplace. She had banned all four children from coming there, even Chrys. So the closest she had been to her mother's "home away from home" was sitting behind the windshield of her father's car on days when her mother's Buick was in the shop and they were outside to pick her up. Despite Chrys's nagging each time to let her go inside and get her mother, her father never relented. One of those solemn pacts, Chrys figured, between her parents. Part of Chrys understood her mother's attempt to keep the grimness of life at a distance but another part thought her mother didn't want to admit how mature Chrys was at fifteen. After all, in another six months she would be able to drive her parent's car by herself. And if her mother really thought that

Chrys didn't know anyone who did drugs, she was more naïve than she seemed or should be for a psychologist working in a halfway house. It was just her mother's over-protective nature, Chrys told herself, and though she resented it at times, she couldn't concern herself with it now. She let her huff fume out through her ears and walked toward the grassy area between the two buildings.

The courtyard was cut in half by a brick path that connected two exterior doors and was covered by the third-floor walkway. The rest of it was thick grass and planted beds, well-tended with rose bushes and benches on one side and a few tables and chairs under a large maple tree on the other. It was an area where the occupants and employees could break away from the starkness of the rooms and offices, eat their meals in the fresh air, or smoke to their hearts' content.

Chrys's mother didn't smoke—she denied ever having a desire to—but she said that if addicts hadn't smoked cigarettes before they stopped using drugs, they probably would afterwards. She seemed right about that because her mother's clothes always reeked when she got home, so she'd throw them into the washer and shower as soon as she swept through the back door. As callous as it might sound, kisses and hugs came only after she had washed the day off her skin. Funny, as much as Chrys's mother loved what she did for a living, she wanted none of it to taint her family's lives. So she shared all that was good about it with her children and kept from them everything that wasn't.

Chrys peeked beyond the corner of the building and was relieved to see the last table of folks picking up their lunch trash and preparing to leave. She smiled at the prospect of having total rein over the grounds. Somewhere between these two buildings, maybe under a plant or buried in the earth, was what she was searching for.

The last person to leave was a pleasant-looking woman, a resident, as her blue street dress indicated. Looking as normal as somebody's secretary or some teenager's mother, she threw her trash into a nearby can, snuffed out the stub of her cigarette in a pot of sand by the door and went inside.

Trying to look casual, Chrys strolled into the courtyard. Step by step she scrutinized every inch of earth. Although not quite sure what she was looking for, she was sure she would know it when she saw it. Something out of order, something not quite right would scream at her. A bald patch amidst the grass, perhaps, or a plant's broken branches. On one pass across the grounds she caught a glint among the blades of grass and stooped down only to find that it was a piece of foil wadded into a ball. Another time she stumbled upon something only to discover it was the bulging root of the nearby maple.

Pass after pass she made over that ground, up and down between the twin buildings until she felt she knew every speck of dirt, every twig and blade of grass as well as she did the hundreds of titles in her music collection. After twenty minutes—her neck stiff, her calves scratched, and her knees dimpled from kneeling on the mulch—she put her hands on her hips, sighed with exasperation, and gave up.

As she turned to leave, the door of the first building opened and a grizzled old man stepped out. His hair was dark gray and it stood out in all directions from his head. His eyebrows looked like furry caterpillars hanging over his eyes. He wore a faded green shirt and baggy gray pants and his hand clutched a large, pointed knife with teeth along one edge.

When he caught sight of Chrys, he pointed it at her and barked, "You there, what are you doing here? You're not one of them." And he yanked his thumb toward the building. His eyebrows knitted together into one great woolly bear, and he peered at her intently. With his neck craned outward he stepped in her direction. "You look familiar to me...."

Chrys backed up. He took another step toward her and waved the weapon. Her heart began to pound. She swallowed hard and said, "I ... I ... nothing. Really, I wasn't doing anything."

He rushed toward her. "You shouldn't be here. Why I ought to—"

By this time Chrys had matched his steps in reverse and backed up to the front of the two buildings. Her heel bumped the edge of the walkway, and despite her attempt to regain her balance, she totally lost it. When her backside hit the concrete, she saw the man's eyes grow fierce and determined, and his pace toward her quickened even more.

"You stay away from me!" Chrys yelled.

Shaking, she scrambled to her feet. The man, almost to her now, thrust out his hairy hand at her. Suddenly, the front door of the building swung open and her mother, finishing a conversation with someone inside, stepped sideways out of the door. The man, seeing her, stopped short, smiled at Chrys then disappeared around the corner of the building. Her mother swung around, glared at Chrys and descended the three steps with a slow heaviness. Chrys ran over and threw her arms around her.

"Oh, Mom, a man! A strange man! He was going to kill me!"

"What man?" She put Chrys at arms' length and with a suspicious look said, "What did he look like?"

Chrys pointed to where the killer had disappeared. "He was old and he was wearing an old green shirt and he came at me with a huge knife!"

"Did he have big bushy eyebrows?"

"Yes! How did you know?" Chrys wondered whether

her mother had miraculously been endowed with ESP over her lunchtime cup of tea. Her mother smiled, and Chrys felt even more confused.

"What exactly did he do or say?"

"He asked me why I was here and then he came at me."

"Honey, that was Melvin, our handyman. He's totally harmless. Well, I wouldn't say totally." Chrys clutched her mother again. "What I mean is he's always butting in and ordering people around. We've all learned to ignore him."

"But he was carrying a big knife."

"Chrys, I want you to know how proud I am that you're aware of your surroundings. And that you acted carefully. But sometimes things aren't as they seem. That was no knife. It was a small saw he uses for pruning limbs."

She gently led Chrys around the corner of the building. There across the courtyard was Melvin on a ladder vigorously sawing through a dead branch.

"See?" her mother said and then her voice became stern. "Now then, what possible explanation can you give me for being here?"

Chrys wondered the same thing of her mother. "Why are *you* here? Aren't you supposed to be at lunch?"

"You know better than to answer my question with a question."

Chrys whined, "I'm fifteen, almost sixteen. Why can't I come here?"

"That's *another* question." Then she sighed. "I've explained my reasons to you a hundred times." Once more she took a deep breath and put her hands on Chrys's arms. "Okay, obviously it's really important to you to know where I work. So I'll tell you what I'll do—this fall when it's 'Take Your Daughter to Work Day,' you can spend it here with me. All right?"

Chrys was absolutely ecstatic for this twist in the

conversation, but she put on her pouty mouth, looked down at the ground and pawed at the grass with her foot. "Oh, all right."

Her mother gave her a quick hug. "Good. I'll see you at home later." And with her arm around Chrys's waist she directed her away from the building.

After a few paces Chrys turned around and asked, "Mom, why *are* you here at noon?"

Her mother stopped and as if to lay the whole scene to rest said, "Emergency. But it's over now." She eyed Chrys critically. "Are we okay now? Can I go to lunch without having to worry?"

Chrys nodded and walked on. Her mother, instead of going back inside, waited on the steps until Chrys had reached the traffic light at the end of the street. Chrys didn't mind getting shooed away. She had accomplished what she had gone there to do. Or rather, not. She could barely admit that she could be such a loser. She had never failed in anything she had attempted: ice skating, guitar lessons, and though Peri was smarter in school than she was, she even did well in science. But all these were things she had a passion to do and they were calculated, formulaic—unlike guessing games. Oh, how could New Life Habitat not be what Uncle Jules referred to when he said to find two homes connected by sorrow. What else could he have possibly meant? Chrys shook her head with rebellious impatience and ordered her feet to fly her home where in her room she could bury her thoughts in her music. She turned the corner and in the next few blocks breezed past the items in the shop windows—the treasure chest, the pot of fake coins, and the emerald necklace—without giving them a moment's glance. She had misread all the signs. She thrust her hands into her pockets and vowed that she was done for the day—maybe forever—with riddles.

Coming upon the corner where she would make a right turn toward the library, she literally ran into the Malicious Musketeers rounding the corner from the other direction. Remembering the way she looked before leaving the house, she put her head down like a quarterback and shot to the side as though doing so would make her invisible to them.

"Well, Chrysler," said Jack smiling, "where are you off to in such a hurry? Hey guys, I'll bet she can go zero to sixty in six." All three hooted with laughter.

"None of your business, creep." She tried to scoot around him but he blocked her way.

"Why do you always have to be so defensive?" Jack asked as sincerely as was possible through his snickering. "Chrysler, can't you ever take a simple joke?"

"Not from you." She finally saw a small gap open up between them. Like a bull she put her head down and wishing she had horns, dove through them. A childhood of playing football with her two brothers and the neighborhood boys was more than ample training. When she realized the three weren't following her, she looked around and spouted toward Jack, "And I thought you were the smartest of the three stooges!"

Jack didn't reply. He laughed her off to his friends, but it seemed a nervous laugh to Chrys, and so she trotted off feeling somewhat victorious. Still, she wished he would just leave her alone or at least leave her name alone. It was the one sensitive issue of her life. Why did he have to zero in on that each time? It only served to remind her that she would anguish over it for the rest of her life, though her mother regarded the sound of Chrys's name as a kind of music to her ears.

Her mother had intended to create the perfectly happy home where all four children would blithely bond together. And she believed that storybook home would begin with the names she gave her children and her diligence over the next fifteen years to pull them into an ideal family circle.

Believing her children to be precious, she borrowed their names from what was already precious in her life. Actually, she could have used a great many things as inspiration: she liked to cook and so knew all the famous chefs; she liked her job and her co-workers; she liked painting watercolors and had a collection of books about famous artists. Any one of those interests would have provided a sensible, normal name. But no. Her greatest love in all the world happened to be growing flowers. She never seemed happier than when she was on her hands and knees before her flower beds or arranging a bouquet of cut flowers to adorn that night's dinner or grace her kitchen window sill. She loved so much to see them sprout and bloom that she named each of the children after her absolute favorites.

Chrys had convinced most of her friends and classmates that her name was the result of her mother's poor spelling, but actually Chrys received her name in honor of the hardiness and assertiveness of the chrysanthemum (and from which came Uncle Jules' "Big Flower" joke). Peri came from periwinkle, a highly adaptive flower that grows in all kinds of soils and conditions. Then there was the exotic, almost supernatural beauty of the iris, which became her sister's name. The delicate sweetness of Sweet William became the reason for the other twin's. Thank goodness, Chrys thought, her mother had been considerate enough to make the names sensible on their birth certificates. Maybe, Chrys thought, she should also be more grateful that her mother chose the flowers that she did. After browsing one day through her mother's gardening books, Chrys had become only too aware how much worse her name could be. She could, after all, be sporting one derived from "petunia," or "daffodil," or, heaven help her, "gypsophilia." She cringed in remembering "scabiosa." Still, to be named after a "chrysanthemum..."

She stopped walking and turned around as if she half-expected to see the three boys following her secretly.

"Chrysler," she said to herself. Maybe admitting she was named after a four-wheel drive truck would be easier.

-

CHAPTER 5

The rest of her day was one of total listlessness. She tried to take her mind off the day's events and the disappointment in herself but couldn't. Not even the songs of Dave Matthews or Led Zeppelin helped. None of her friends were home, and TV's seemingly endless choices were mindless. Uncle Jules' mission had become not a monkey on her back, but a silver-backed gorilla.

She had often imagined she knew what addiction was like, especially when her craving for dark chocolate consumed her every thought. But now she truly understood the power of obsession. She didn't know how she was going to figure out her uncle's riddle, but she would wait forever, if she had to, for a sign.

Coming through the kitchen doorway, her mother called for help with dinner. Chrys got up from the couch with a subtle sense of renewed self-worth and moseyed into the dining room. The twins clattered down the stairs arguing over who should fill the water glasses and who should put out the silverware and napkins. Chrys rolled her eyes at them, called them "children" and went into the kitchen to offer her mother help with last minute details.

"Ugh," she said eyeing the pot roast on the stove and immediately hoped her mother at the sink washing her hands hadn't heard her. Chrys had thought the pleasant smell throughout the house for the last hour or so was stew.

Her mother dried her hands and then called the others

to dinner. Chrys picked up a plate from the stack and slipped a small piece of the roast onto it then buried the meat with veggies and potatoes. At the dinner table she put her face in her hands to brace herself for the meal. She knew she didn't have to eat what her mother made; she could always pick at what she liked and then make a PB & J. But she saw how tired her mother looked and Chrys didn't want to add any more fullness to her mother's already puffy face or irritation to her voice after what had happened in town earlier. Chrys would suffer through the pot roast for her mother's sake—and for just a smidgen of her own. With little sleep herself, even two slabs of bread with a simple smear of peanut butter between them seemed just too dangerous. What if she should go narcoleptic while making that sandwich and fall face down on the counter with a knife in her hand? Two deaths in the family within a week would definitely dry her mother's tear ducts to blindness.

Her father sat at the end of the table. The four children filled in the side seats. As usual Chrys parked herself next to Iris and across from Peri. Her mother would sit at the opposite end. No sooner did her father get settled comfortably into his chair and sneaked a sample bite but Iris kicked William under the table. Whether she did accidentally or not, William kicked her back.

Not able to swallow fast enough to speak, her father rapped his fork several times on the side of his plate as a judge raps his gavel for order in the courtroom.

He took a quick sip of water then said, "Keep your feet under your chairs. Let's try to make this meal as peaceful as possible."

Perhaps, Chrys thought, her mother had tried too hard with the children. Despite her mother's best efforts and wishes and wisdom, they could not have been more disconnected. It wasn't that they hated one another, although at times they did; it's just that they weren't remotely close, even the twins. Chrys often wondered how agonized and guilty her mother must have felt about her children growing up as strangers to one other. After all, she was a highly respected therapist in Willow who had all kinds of success mending the fabric of people's problems except when it came to tightening the weave of her own children's lives. Sometimes, Chrys suspected that the children's indifference and especially their animosity to one another killed their mother. She would get all teary-eyed and her lips would quiver and then she would break into the story of how she had named each of them. But after the additional tears her mother had recently shed over Uncle Jules, Chrys vowed to curb her irritation with her brothers and sister—that is, when her mother was within earshot.

Finally, her mother came out of the kitchen and sat down with her plate. Then she turned to Chrys. "Now, whatever is so unpleasant about pot roast that you have to make that awful sound and wear that awful face every time I make it?"

With her fork Chrys picked apart the layers of the chuck roast on her plate then held up a grayish mass clinging to the tines. "The taste is all right," she said to soften the blow. "It's this Gothic slime." And she scraped the gummy lump onto the edge of her plate. "'Quoth the raven: Nevermore!'"

Her mother's eyes welled up with tears. She snatched up her napkin and sniffled into it. "Julius used to say that...."

"Sorry, Mom," Chrys quickly said. "I didn't mean to upset you."

"Yes, you did," Peri said. "All you ever care about is yourself."

"That's not true," Chris snapped. "And look who's talking—the wanna-be egghead who thinks he's going to Hah-vaad Law School."

"Before they'll ever open the door with welcome arms for *you*."

"Enough," her father sternly said. He didn't have to say, "Not another word."

Chrys mumbled, "He started it," to be on record.

Her father eyed her and Peri as though he could burn holes through their skulls then he glanced at the twins, too. "These last few days have been rough on everyone. So each of you—choose your words carefully." He looked around the table again. Iris was sticking her tongue out at William, who glared back at her and opened his mouth to speak. Her father blurted, "That was not a suggestion."

A long pause followed but eventually the clinking of silverware and glasses settled the air back to normalcy— silent hostility. Chrys debated about sharing her uncle's nighttime visitation. After her miserable failure to locate the "houses that aren't houses" and without a clue of where to look next, she figured her mother might be the one to help. Uncle Jules was her mother's brother, so maybe there was something her mother would understand from his message that was lost on Chrys. Taking a nibble of the roast without wincing, she said, "Uncle Jules visited me last night."

"Oh Honey," her mother said and looked at Chrys in the same worrisome way when she had explained there was no Santa. She reached over and gently stroked Chrys's hair. "It's okay. I've been dreaming of him too."

Chrys looked up at her. "It wasn't a dream, Mom. He was there at the foot of my bed."

"Now I know how much you love your uncle..." She looked around at the shocked and gaping expressions of the other three children. "...but you're scaring the twins."

Peri, Iris and William closed their mouths and simultaneously looked down. As if rehearsed, they jabbed at their food with their forks and pushed pieces of it around in circles on their plates.

As usual, Chrys was all by herself. None of them ever sided with her, or with each other for that matter. Why in the world would she expect them to support her now when she had just proclaimed she'd seen her dead uncle? After all, what teen, or almost teen—other than her—would risk having her parents add the label of "mental defective" to the already "hormonal mess?" Still, Chrys was no liar and the four of them were supposed to be "kindred spirits." That was her mother's expression. Over the years she had slipped it into every conversation she could—the same way she dropped an extra teaspoon of sugar into her coffee when no one was looking—in still another attempt to sweeten her children's relationships.

Chrys watched her brothers and sister at the table still moving pieces of meat around their plates like they were choreographing the Ice Capades. More and more, no matter how loony Chrys had sounded, she resented their silence. Fine, she thought. So be it. Why bother any of their feeble little minds with it. As usual, she felt like an "only child" who would have to depend on her own resources to carry out the greatest and yet most frustrating mystery of her life.

The evening hours passed for Chrys with still more listlessness. Even the Sci-fi Channel, "Iron Chef America" or MTV couldn't remove it. Plagued with a fresh sense of failure, she found another wave of resentment creeping into her thoughts, but not toward herself or even her brothers and sister. This time, it was directed toward Uncle Jules. He had given her an impossible assignment. Why would he have toyed with her fond memory of him so? Why hadn't he simply told her where to go to and what to do? And how in the world could she find out that information now? Gaining help from the family had dead-ended when they refused even to believe Uncle Jules had visited her. She sighed, dug a deeper trench for herself in the couch and clicked through more channels.

A few minutes later she heard her brothers coming down the stairs talking about playing pool. William sailed past her on his way to the basement, but Peri stopped behind the couch where she was lying.

"So how did Uncle Jules appear to you?" Peri whispered smiling. "Did he come through the wall like he did with me? What exactly did he say to you?"

Chrys's heart skipped a beat. Uncle Jules visited Peri, too? And then she registered what he was doing. It was just another of his sick jokes played on her. Well, she wasn't about to let him get away with it. She peered up at him and narrowed her eyes like a cobra's.

"He told me," she said snidely, "that I shouldn't give an alien the time of day, who even with three heads doesn't know when to keep his mouth shut around his grieving mother."

"All right. I can take a subtle hint. I guess next year then, with my lips sealed, you won't be bugging me for help with organic chem." He leaned over the back of the couch. "Besides," he said as snidely as she had, "you're the one who made her cry." And he smugly trotted off to the basement.

She could have screamed at him across the house like a banshee for that, but she had made a vow to restrain herself and would stick to it. While her hand scrolled through the channels, her mind scrolled through what Peri had said. Suddenly, she realized there was someone other than her parents and siblings who could help her. She recalled the Ouija board, which her new ESP book confirmed as a genuine tool. Was it buried somewhere in her closet? Or was it under her bed? Then she remembered Peri borrowing it a couple weeks ago for a sleepover. Getting it back could be tricky, she thought, because Peri's smarts made him a dyedin-the-wool snoop. She desperately wanted to get Uncle Jules to return and supply her with the answers to all her questions. But based on her disaster at dinner, she knew to try that alone. Peri and Iris and William might have said nothing at the table, yet they had laughed at her just the same. And way before dinner she had already tired of being a laughing stock.

Still, she fought tooth and nail with herself. She repeatedly weighed her goal of contacting Uncle Jules against her hatred for puzzles and the probability that he wouldn't share more—after all, he loved to keep people guessing. Still, the fact that she had a strategy at all bolstered her confidence.

The clock on the mantle chimed ten. Her parents were in the den across the house, her mother no doubt reading in one overstuffed chair while her father, given the time, was probably napping in the other. Peri and William were still in the basement playing pool, and she was certain they would be down there a good deal longer. They had just come upstairs minutes before, like taking a breath after being submerged, and raided snacks from the pantry.

Chrys pulled herself off the couch and headed up the steps, hoping Iris had also secluded herself. With fingers crossed what Chrys really hoped was that her sister had locked herself in the bathroom upstairs. Recently, before getting into the shower, Iris had begun to play with the makeup kit Chrys had gotten from her mother for Christmas. Out of principle Chrys always yelled at Iris to keep out of it, but when she was really sleepy, the principle of keeping Iris out of things Chrys couldn't care less about just wasn't worth escalating into an all-out war. Now standing at the bathroom door, she actually prayed that Iris had ignored her wishes.

As carefully as she could, she tried the bathroom door,

but the knob made a slight click.

"I'm showering!" Iris shouted. And then the sound of the water started up.

"All right, all right," Chrys said beaming and quickly backed up. "I'll use the downstairs bathroom."

She bumped into something small and hard. After her earlier bruising at the halfway house, she winced. Turning, she saw it was a doorknob and not, thank goodness, Peri wielding his infernal flashlight. She glanced toward the stairs, tried to stand as still and unassuming as a fire hydrant to make sure no one was coming, then slipped into the room and clicked on the small light at Peri's desk. Where should she start looking for the Ouija board was a problem since the room looked like someone had ransacked it. Locating it would have been easy if the boys housed board games in one place, books in another and Lego collections elsewhere. But both were pathetic slobs and so the Ouija board could be anywhere: buried in the closet, at the bottom of a drawer, or—she prayed not—shoved high onto the closet shelf where at five-foot-four she was too short to reach it.

Panicking that she'd been there too long already, she moved like a ghost about the room, disturbing as little as possible and making sure she returned everything to its original position, even though she had plucked it out of perfect chaos. After she had gone through every eye-level shelf, she got down on all fours and spun in a circle. Finally, she spotted the box under Peri's bed. She reached in, nervously aware of the friendly environment for spiders the boys' room provided, grabbed the corner of the box, and as slickly as an eel slithered out from under the bed with it. She could tell from the clunk when she picked it up that the stylus was inside. She turned out the light and sped to her room. Hearing her parents on the stairs, she slipped the box under her bed then threw herself onto it and picked up a book from the nightstand. Her mother didn't believe in contact with the spirit world and though she hadn't forbidden the Ouija board, she wasn't exactly keen about it either. And given what Chrys had said at dinner, her mother would most likely guess correctly about what she was trying to do. Then with tears, many more tears, her mother would engage her in an hour-long heart-to-heart talk.

Chrys heard her parents murmuring to each other as they passed her door. She propped up on her forearms and read distractedly for several agonizing minutes, then unable to overcome the urge to contact her uncle, she set up the Ouija board, lit the candle and turned out the lights. In total darkness a single candle, she hoped, like a beacon from a lighthouse, would bring Uncle Jules to her again. As she placed her hands lightly on the stylus, there came a tapping. She immediately thought of "The Raven."

Slipping into Poe's literary skin, she recited, "As of someone gently rapping, rapping at my chamber door—" In the pause that followed Chrys imagined with wild anticipation that it might be Uncle Jules.

"Chrys, may I come in?"

Chrys's musing evaporated. It was her mother's voice. She shoved the Ouija board so hard under the bed that the stylus tumbled into the wall on the other side of her bed. She prayed she hadn't broken it. Then without a protest from Chrys, her mother opened the door and stepped in.

"I wanted to say goodnight," she said gently.

She stopped a few feet from the door and studied Chrys, who was sitting on the floor and staring at the flickering candle.

"Are you all right?" her mother asked.

"I'm fine. Just thinking."

Her mother approached her and kissed her cheek. "Well, there's certainly nothing wrong with that. But if you ever need to talk..."

"I know." Chrys said and nodded. But she knew her mother meant "talk to me instead of ghosts."

Her mother nodded in return, kissed her on the forehead and quietly left, closing the door so slowly that the latch barely clicked. Chrys breathed a sigh of relief, blew out the candle and clicked on the bedside lamp. After that she bided her time by listening to music and writing in her journal. She would take no more chances.

By midnight Iris's light was out and the boys had shuffled upstairs and hunkered down in their room. Still, she did not set up the Ouija board. She had remembered to lock her door to give the spirit world uninterrupted silence and her utter concentration. So only when the light under Peri and William's door was extinguished did she inspect the stylus for damage, wriggle under the bed to retrieve the Ouija board and light the candle. She sat cross-legged in front of it, leaned forward and lightly placed her fingers on the stylus. After a few seconds of stillness, it began to glide slowly across the surface.

As though she had dialed his phone number, she whispered, "Are you there Uncle Jules? Oh, please answer."

CHAPTER 6

Chrys closed her eyes as the stylus moved across the board. She knew better than to jinx the results by watching it. Some people, like her mother, doubted that the source of the message could be a spirit, believing instead that the person's subconscious guided the object. So Chrys eliminated any possibility of that theory by closing her eyes until the stylus stopped on the board.

The first time she used the Ouija that way, she had communicated with a three-year-old girl. Chrys questioned how such a little child was able to write, and the girl answered that a ten-year-old boy was spelling for her. Chrys was immediately reminded of an Alex Haley quote from Uncle Jules: "If you see a turtle on top of a fence post, you know he had some help." Before talking to that girl, Chrys thought the quote applied only to famous rock stars who couldn't sing. But the young girl's comment touched her so much that Chrys teared up, and so she asked the girl if she regretted leaving the earth. The girl replied that she had not been there long enough to miss it. Well, those words not only made Chrys bawl her eyes dry but convinced her that no matter what her mother believed, she had truly been in touch with the afterworld. Even so, she was so depressed that she had gladly loaned the Ouija board to Peri.

The stylus meandering about the board suddenly stopped. Chrys opened her eyes, saw the letter "Y" through the glass circle then tightly shut her eyes again when the stylus jerked into motion. The next letter was "O." Then a minute later came "U." Chris smiled and silently thanked her uncle for coming to her rescue. A string of others, "A-R-E-A-L-L" came more slowly. Every part of her tingled. "You are all..." she repeated as the stylus swung down and far right across the board before it halted. Chrys opened her eyes to see it parked over blank space. Just a spasm in the transmission, she thought. Messages from the other world ran into glitches almost as often as they did across the Internet, although she wondered for a moment whether Uncle Jules was having second thoughts. She closed her eyes again. "Please, please, please" ran in her head as she patiently waited.

A few seconds later, the stylus lurched into action. "Y-O-U" spelled out again and Chrys hoped Uncle Jules wasn't experiencing some kind of supernatural tic that would repeat over and over again like a scratched record on a phonograph used to do. But then an "N" followed and in rapid succession "E-E-D."

"You are all you need," Chrys whispered aloud but was disheartened in the long pause that followed to think that was the end of the message. She stared at the stylus. "This isn't a lesson on Hamlet, is it? 'To thine own self be true,' or something like that?" She leaned back, looked up and whined, "Uncle Jules, won't you help me?"

Several minutes passed with her fingers on the stylus but it didn't move. She placed it on another spot on the board and tried again. It didn't budge. A third try proved as unsuccessful. Not ready to give up, she constructed a question that required a simple "yes" or "no" answer. Her lips opened to pose it to Uncle Jules when again came a tapping on her door. Added to it this time, though, was a glow under the door.

Chrys felt a chill run over her body as fast as a runaway

train and expected Uncle Jules to seep through her door in all his blue-haze glory. Instead, the doorknob clicked and a much higher voice than her uncle's said, "Chrys, let me in."

Recognizing Peri's voice, she said, "What do *you* want?"

"Have you seen the Ouija board?"

She got up and came to the door but didn't open it. "Why?"

"It's not under my bed."

"So?"

"Aw come on. Do you have it?"

"What if I do?"

There was a pause and then Peri whispered through the crack of the door, "Open up, will you? I've got to tell you something."

Chrys turned the lock and opened the door a few inches. With his flashlight in hand, Peri peered at her then at the Ouija board on the floor.

"I wasn't teasing you earlier. I really did see Uncle Jules."

Chrys opened the door a bit wider. "So? Maybe Mom's right and you just dreamed about him."

"No. I saw him with my eyes wide open."

Chrys swung the door wide, put her finger to her lips to keep him from jabbering on, then closed the door after him.

"All right," she said skeptically. She was thinking how much more she'd dislike Peri if he was playing an abominably insensitive joke on her on the heels of her uncle's death.

Peri leaned against the door and hung his head. "Really, Chrys, last night he came as a blue light through the wall."

Chrys, still suspicious, asked, "What was he wearing?'"

"A T-shirt ... with a quote from Shakespeare. I don't remember which one."

"Did William see him too?"

"He was upstairs in bed. I was watching a movie in the living room when all of a sudden he came through the wall."

Guardedly Chrys asked, "Did he talk to you?"

"Not for very long. He said he came back to ask me to do something for him. To find a treasure and take it to its owner."

Chrys could barely keep her skin on. She desperately wanted to believe Peri's story but before she could, she tried to calculate what the odds were to fabricate a story like that. Peri was smart, highly inventive. Could he have taken what she said at dinner and come up with something as hare-brained and coincidental as that off the top of his head? After all, Uncle Jules had several shirts with Shakespearean quotes on them. How convenient that Peri didn't recall which one. But then again Peri was no fan of Shakespeare since he always referred to him as the "Barf of Avon."

"So how are you supposed to find the treasure?" Chrys asked.

"He told me I'd need to find 'a park that's not a park.'"

She grabbed his arm and practically shrieked, "You *are* telling me the truth!"

This detail was just too creepy for her to continue to doubt him. The odds that he made that up were too close to getting bit by a shark in Lake Erie.

But Peri looked hurt. "What did you think? That I'd honestly pull some morbid stunt after Uncle Jules' death? Shows how human you think I am."

"Okay, okay." She took a deep breath and waited for his face to soften. "Listen, Uncle Jules said exactly the same thing to me. Well, almost exactly. He gave me a different clue, 'two houses that aren't houses, ones connected by great sorrow.'"

"Wow, what does that mean? Or what he told me? That it would 'benefit someone in need.' And why did we get

42

different clues?" One of his eyebrows raised. "Maybe there's more than one treasure."

"Gee, I hadn't thought of that." Reluctantly she added, "Good point."

She walked over to the candle and sat down on the floor in front of it. Peri joined her. The candlelight made his face look more manly. At five-foot-ten he was sure to be as tall as their father when he finished growing, but his body and face weren't chiseled yet. The light, however, threw shadows on his face that gave Chrys an idea of his great potential. With his unfreckled face, his height and his brain, he could very well be even more obnoxious in a couple years than he was at the present.

"Hey," he said sliding the stylus back and forth across the board, "maybe we can contact Uncle Jules again."

"That's why you came looking for this, huh?"

"And that's why you sneaked into my room to get it, huh?"

The coincidence was too bizarre for them both not to chuckle, but then she grew solemn. "I've already tried. All he said was, 'You are all you need.' But how can I do this all by myself? I mean, I tried to find those houses today. I thought he meant the two buildings at New Life Habitat."

Peri's eyes lit up. "Of course, the halfway house. Makes perfect sense." He looked askance at her as though hoping she didn't catch his compliment. "You didn't find anything there?"

"Nope, but... " Her eyebrows arched. "I did find Mom."

"Ouch." Peri sat down on the bed. "You know, I spent the day looking, too. I went to Chestnut Park. Nothing. I went to the Little League Park. Nothing. Then Eat and Park. Not a thing, except I did find the hamburger and chocolate shake to be quite a treasure."

They both laughed again. Then Peri recited, "'You are

43

all you need.' Chrys, maybe that doesn't mean what you think it does."

"What else... "But she was interrupted by two soft knocks on the door.

"Can I come in?" William asked.

Chrys looked at Peri and put her finger to her lips. Peri nodded.

"Why not," Chrys said opening the door. "It's suddenly Grand Central."

William stepped into the room, his light brown hair a collage of numerous clumps and his pajamas mismatched. He was the perfect denizen, Chrys thought, for that ghetto across the hall her brothers called a room.

William's eyes locked onto the Ouija board. "Are you using that?"

"Since when are you interested in the spirit world?" Chrys asked.

William's eyes grew wide and he whispered, "Since Uncle Jules came to see me last night."

Chrys's eyes shot daggers at Peri and then at William. "Both of you cold-blooded toads, get out of here!" She stood and yanked at Peri to get up. "Have your laughs in your own room."

"What's going on?" William asked.

"She thinks you and I are playing a prank on her." Peri said.

"Why would you think that, Chrys?" William said.

"Because Peri just told me some far-fetched story about Uncle Jules visiting him." She shoved William closer to the door. "But the joke's over now, ha ha, so leave." She yanked Peri's arm to get him off her bed. She stomped to the door and grabbed the doorknob to usher them out, but it turned automatically in her hand.

A small voice said, "Can I come in?"

The door opened and Iris slipped in. She seemed surprised to see Peri and William there.

In the same small voice she said to Chrys, "I wanted to talk to you. About what you said at dinner."

"Oh, don't tell me." Chrys said rolling her eyes. "Uncle Jules visited you last night."

Iris looked shocked and she swallowed hard. "How did you know?"

Chrys opened her mouth to jump on the boys for putting Iris up to that, but Iris's thin voice continued, so eerily that Chrys couldn't speak.

"He was blue," Iris said, "and he was wearing the shirt that says, 'Doubt truth to be a liar; But never doubt I love." She burst into tears. "He didn't look or sound sad," she blurted through her sobs, "but I could tell he was."

"Well, I'll be..." Peri said.

Chrys offered no more protests, not after hearing from Iris, who was the last person on the planet to play jokes on others. Waiflike, she was the most timid of the four. What was funny was that her big exotic eyes and spooky intuition often intimidated Peri and William as they seemed to be at this moment. They stared at her with mouths gaping. And no one budged; no one said a word; no one even blinked. The boys might be rattled, Chrys thought, but she felt envious of Iris's sixth sense perception.

Finally, Iris broke the silence. "I tried all day to figure out his riddle, but I just couldn't." And another stream of tears rolled down her face.

Chrys felt her own eyes welling up. "Let's sit down and see if we can figure this out."

They sat in a circle around the candle and each told their story of Uncle Jules' visitation, making sure not to leave anything out and recalling verbatim as much as they could. Chrys recounted her story first, then Peri. William, next, added the riddle of finding "a horn that isn't a horn." He said he had thought of horn toads and hornbills, but Ohio had none of those. And then there was the horn of plenty, the one their mother used at Thanksgiving but was now stored in the basement. When he had found it, though, it was empty. Iris, on the other hand, had been instructed to locate "a school which isn't a school" and had thought of a school of fish. So she had investigated the large aquarium in the house of a friend who was Uncle Jules' neighbor. She also checked out her blackboard in the basement where she played school. Then she had a hunch that he might have meant "Skool" because she had heard of a musical group with that word in their name. When she called Aunt Lydia and asked if Uncle Jules had been interested in anything like that, Aunt Lydia said she doubted if he'd ever invest time in anything misspelled. Iris sighed in finishing her story of a dead-end day, and the four of them exchanged puzzled glances.

"We're no further ahead," said Peri. "Even I can't figure out what we're supposed to do."

"Even you? What are *we*, chopped liver?" Chrys said.

"Oh, so I suppose you've got it all figured out," Peri snapped back.

"Hey," Chrys said, "we're not even sure we're talking about one mission."

Peri's eyes glowed. "Oh yes we are. 'You are all you need.' I've got it! He meant 'you' plural! He was saying that the four of us are all we need."

"And what's the connection between a house, park, horn, and school that really aren't any of those things?" Chrys waited for her brilliant brother to supply the answer.

Iris piped up in her little voice, "I have a feeling that the order of his visits might be important. I mean, he did make a point of getting to all of us in one night."

"Okay," William said, "do all of you remember the time he visited you?"

Chrys said three a. m. Peri claimed eleven p. m. Iris said she had come upstairs after a favorite TV program ended at ten-thirty and when she got to her room, Uncle Jules was waiting inside. William, a light sleeper, said he'd heard his parents in the hall at six a. m., groaned at being awakened and then saw the room go blue. Throughout the whole time, Peri had slept on, even afterwards when William shook him roughly.

"You need to work on waking up," William said frowning.

"Yeah, like I can. Or want to," Peri said.

"What if the house was on fire?"

"Oh pa-lease, children," Chrys said yawning.

"Yeah," said William, "we need to get to the bottom of this tonight. I can't wait to get my hands on that treasure."

"Oh so now you're a *greedy* little toad," Chrys said. "Uncle Jules specifically said it was to go to its rightful owner."

"Well, for all this mental work and who knows how much physical work this is going to take, I think I deserve a reward."

"You're pathetic," Chrys said. "You can stay up all night thinking about this if you want to, Willy-boy." She yawned again. "As for me, I'm going to bed."

"Me too," Iris added getting up.

"But we've got all the information," William said. "School, then park, house and horn."

"Just remember," Chrys said, "there are two 'houses' to fit into that list."

"Tomorrow," Peri said authoritatively as he walked toward the door with Iris.

William grudgingly got up and followed Iris out. Then

Peri swung the door shut behind him. But before it clicked, he opened it again.

"Chrysler."

"Where did you...?" Chrys sputtered.

"Eat and Park," he said smirking. "It's the place to discover—if not Uncle Jules' treasure—then some other real beautes."

Backing away, he bowed in a gentlemanly fashion as he closed the door but then snickered all the way to his room. Chrys couldn't move or speak. All she could do was boil over with the notion of living with that name now under her own roof.

Jack, she vowed, would pay dearly for that.

CHAPTER 7

Chrys slowly spooned oatmeal into her mouth while staring at the closed phonebook on the kitchen table in front of her. Then she turned her head and read the clock on the microwave. Ten thirty-six. Where were they? She had awakened Iris and William—and tried to jostle Peri—almost a half hour ago. She jabbed her spoon again into her bowl and took another mouthful. With her other hand she pulled the Willow Telephone Directory closer and opened it to the "S's." Her fingers lingered for a moment but instead of flipping through the pages, she snapped the book shut and pushed it away. Again she gazed at the clock. Was she the only one who took Uncle Jules seriously? Licking the back of the spoon, she saw William out of the corner of her eye zip through the kitchen doorway. He was dressed in khaki shorts and a clean t-shirt and his whole head of sandy brown hair was actually going in the right directions.

"Okay," he said rubbing his hands together, "let's find that treasure." He opened the pantry and grabbed a box of cereal, then milk from the fridge, and a bowl from the cupboard. "I've got my Christmas-in-June list all ready."

"I told you. We're not keeping whatever we find."

"But there has to be something in it for us." He smiled at her, sat down at the table, and took a heaping spoon of cereal. "Don't worry," he said crunching. "You can even have a bigger portion than the rest of us."

"That's not the same as offering me the largest piece of

pie. Oh, I know," she reiterated a standard line of his, "you'd gladly give me the shirt off your back. But this time it doesn't belong to you. And besides, Material Boy, the last thing you need is still another possession to call your own."

"Hey, if I'm the Material Boy then you're the Material Girl. Go look at your CD and book collections."

"Yes, but that's art. You collect nothing but junk, from senseless designer clothes to worthless baseball cards to soulless video games."

Before he could swallow and speak, Iris appeared at the door looking worried.

"Where's Peri?" Chyrs asked.

"He's still asleep."

"Still asleep! Where's a stick of dynamite to light underneath him? So he wants to wander off to Andromeda in his dreams, does he? Well, I'd gladly send him there for real!"

Swallowing a last mouthful, William launched out of his chair. "Hey, Chrys, don't bust a lung over Peri. It's simple. The three of us will go. I'm ready." And he rubbed his hands together again and started out the door.

"Stop William," Chrys called. "Come back here. We've got to do this together. Uncle Jules planned it that way. I thought we all decided that last night."

William swung around and stomped back, his hands in his pockets. Chrys noticed that Iris hadn't budged or blinked since she entered the kitchen. And her brow was even more deeply knitted.

"What's the matter?" Chrys asked.

"I ... I don't think I want to go."

Chrys got up, put her bowl in the sink, and came over to her. "Why not?" She rested her hand on Iris's shoulder and felt her shudder. "You're spooked over this, aren't you?"

"I think I'm getting sick," Iris said.

50

"Oh my gosh," William whined. "She's creeped herself out again. And she didn't even use the Ouija board last night. Or watch a ghost story."

Chrys shot William a look of exasperation. "And 'Oh my gosh.' We're only living one, pea-head."

"Low blow. You don't have to call me a pea-head."

"I really don't feel good," Iris said growing pale. She wheezed slightly and headed for a chair where she pulled out her inhaler from her jacket pocket. She put the end in her mouth, pressed down on the top, and administered the customary whoosh of medication.

Chrys walked over and put her hand on Iris's forehead. "You don't feel hot." She knelt down to look at Iris eye to eye. "We've got to do this together or it won't work. Iris, you can do this, "she said as sincerely as she could, though she resented the times like this when she felt compelled to baby Iris out of a full-blown asthma attack. She had felt differently when Iris was little, but as time went on and Iris entered middle school, Chrys expected her to grit her teeth and deal with things the way Chrys did. "Maybe you'll feel better if you have some breakfast." Chrys rose and went to the refrigerator. "I'll make you something, okay? One bagel with cream cheese and strawberry jam, coming up." She glanced back at Iris who nodded faintly but still didn't look reassured. Chrys sliced the bagel and put the halves in the toaster. "And we'll make sure to take plenty of water. Maybe we should pack a lunch in case we have to make a day of it. We can stop somewhere really pretty. Okay Iris?"

"Take along where?" William asked. "Do you have any idea where we're going?"

"Not exactly," Chrys said slathering the bagel with cream cheese and jam and then licking her fingers, "but I thought we could start with the phonebook."

"For what?" Peri said from the doorway. He hiked up

51

his pajama bottoms higher on his hips, retied them and then ran his fingers through his hair.

Chrys eyed her brother narrowly. Then her eyes shot to the clock and back again to him.

"Oh shut up," he said opening the refrigerator.

"It's been an hour since I woke everyone up. And knowing you, it'll be another hour before you're ready to leave.

"What's an hour," he said grabbing the carton of orange juice. "Or two? The treasure's not going anywhere. Quit nagging me." He looked at her meanly. "Where'd you get that annoying little habit? Mom's no nag." He slouched back against the counter and took a swig.

"I'm no nag." Chrys glanced at Iris and hoped this delay wouldn't change her sister's fragile state of mind—or healthy constitution. "You're just a jerk."

"Besides," Peri said snatching up the other half of the prepared bagel and carrying it over to the table, "where is it we're headed? I'm assuming you have that figured out. Or maybe Iris is going to lay hands on the phonebook and supernaturally 'read' where we're supposed to go." He took a big bite out of the bagel, leaving a huge red smile that made him resemble the Joker from *Superman*. Chrys found the look quite fitting. She bit her lip to keep from laughing and tipping him off, but he licked his lips and quickly erased all trace of his alter ego. Then she looked at Iris who had shrunk into a little ball in her seat.

Glancing back at Peri, Chrys said, "You know, you really shouldn't open your mouth until you've made sure it's connected to your brain." But she didn't wait for a response. Instead, she quickly breezed on in an attempt to bulldoze Iris out of her panic. "If we are to find a school that's not a school then what better place to start our search but in the phonebook. Maybe there are businesses, like a dog

52

obedience school, or people's names..." And she opened the book to the "S's." She found the page and read aloud, "Schook, David. School Board of Evergreen County—See Government Section. Schooley, Heather. School—See Individual Names." More slowly she read, "Schoonheim, Sheldon." She looked up at them and shut the book.

"What're you stopping for?" William asked.

Chrys spelled, "S-c-h-o-o-n. Get it?"

"Well, that's that," Iris said, her brow smooth again.

But Chrys was not about to abandon their goal. She sat down, rested her head in her hands and glared at Peri. William followed suit.

"What'll we do now, O Wise One?" she said.

Peri drummed his fingers on the tabletop and stared at the phonebook as though he were blessed with telekinesis and could command it to fly open on its own and point the way. He tipped his chair back and ran his hand through his hair then over his face. Finally, a grin stretched out almost as far as the strawberry one had.

"Well, we could always go to Buckeye High and snoop around," he said.

Chrys kowtowed at him. "O Gray Matter Master, and what's the use in going there?" She sat up straight and as though she were talking to a small child, said, "That's a real school. We're supposed to be looking for an un-real school."

Peri ignored her and directed his explanation to the twins. "Maybe something on the school grounds where Uncle Jules used to teach will fit the riddle."

William bounded from his seat and slid his hands over one another. "Works for me."

Chrys said. "That sounds like one heck of a long shot."

"Me too," said Iris, her body coiling up again.

Peri leaned over the table. "Why wouldn't Uncle Jules take us back to the place that meant almost as much to him

53

as home."

"That does make sense," Chrys blurted and then wished she hadn't given her brother credit for the second time in twenty-four hours for having a brain in his head. "All right, everyone, clean up your mess. I'll make some sandwiches. Peri, you try, just try to be ready in half an hour."

She got up and scurried about the kitchen, pulling mustard and ham from the refrigerator and bread from the pantry. Peri deliberately snailed his way across the kitchen. She pushed him hard through the doorway and like a rag doll he flopped onto the dining room floor. It would do no good to humor him or scream at him to hurry. She did, however, glare and growl at him.

Suddenly, a wheeze so loud cut through the air that William stopped loading the dishwasher and Chrys looked back and moaned.

"How are we supposed to go there with Iris's asthma?" said William. "Maple High is twice as far as Willow."

"I know how to get there," Chrys said after a few seconds.

"Taxi?" Peri said standing up. "Only with your money."

"No, I've got a better idea. And cheaper."

She pointed to the garage where her parents' 2004 Jetta resided until it became her 2004 Jetta in ninety-four days when she turned sixteen. Iris's eyes widened with terror. Chrys shot her that "Gee thanks" look. But realizing Iris was genuinely shaken—again—Chrys said, "All back roads, every single one of them. No sweat."

"Unless there are any boulders with a mind to jump out in front of you," Peri said.

"That boulder in the shopping center was sticking way over the curb! And besides, that accident happened my very first week behind the wheel!" She put down the knife, planted her hands on her hips, and flicked her head so that her hair flew behind her shoulders like a startled bird. "Since then I've done fine. Exceptionally even. Dad said so the other day."

"Yeah," Peri smirked, "only after a twenty-minute ride cringing in the passenger seat with his eyes shut." He shot through the house and Chrys, chasing him, hurled the sopping sponge at him that she had snatched from the kitchen sink. He leaped onto the stairs. The sponge, missing him, landed in a silk plant.

"Fifteen minutes, Peri!" she shouted. "Fifteen minutes before we leave without you!"

She plucked the sponge from the pot and returned to the kitchen.

William looked confused. "Leave without Peri? But I thought you said..."

Chrys sighed. "Don't you ever get anything?"

"Sure I do," he said grabbing cans of soda from the refrigerator. "I always get when you're trying to make me feel like an idiot."

CHAPTER 8

Within a miraculous twelve minutes the four of them were out the door. At first Chrys was amazed that her ploy on Peri had worked, but then she second-guessed her ability to trick him, wondering if he wasn't just as anxious as the rest of them to get moving. So maybe it was the other way around; maybe it was Peri who had tricked her with his dawdling attitude. In any case, she was so pleased with his quick appearance, dressed and ready to go, that she could have burst in turning the key in the ignition.

The three others waited outside the cramped garage for her to pull out. She put the gearshift in reverse, but in her excitement to get going and her nervousness to drive without one of her parents, her foot slipped on the clutch and the car lurched backwards. Iris squealed and jumped. William chewed on a fingernail.

"Oh great!" Peri said throwing up his hands. "I didn't know we were putting our lives on the line." He turned and started for the house.

Chrys yelled through the window. "Oh stop it. My foot slipped. Like it's never happened to Mom or Dad." She started the car again. Smoothly, she rolled it the rest of the way out of the garage and swung the back end under the basketball hoop so she could head the car down the driveway.

Peri turned back and shaking his head, sauntered over. After passing Iris and William, he raised his arm and motioned them on. When they got close to the car, William shot in front of Peri as though intercepting a pass and grabbed the front door handle. Peri reached around him and yanked William's hand away.

"Oh no you don't," Peri said. "I ride shotgun. Especially after what just happened."

William frowned. "I always have to ride in the back with Iris."

Iris looked wounded.

"I didn't mean it like that," he said to Iris. "It's just that time that we drove through the Blue Ridge Mountains."

"Yeah, you puked up your guts," Peri said. "But that was two years ago, and you're a big boy now."

William, frowning further, climbed into the back seat.

"Hey," said Chrys, "we have straight roads ahead and me behind the wheel." And she put the car into first and cruised down the driveway.

Her parents had insisted on buying the Jetta, over more desirable cars and way before Chrys turned sixteen, purely because it had manual transmission. At first Chrys thought her dad was concerned with the gas mileage and easier maintenance, but then she overheard him tell her mother that if Chrys had to use both hands to operate it, she wouldn't be able to hold a burger or a cell phone while driving. He hadn't sounded smug exactly, but he did seem proud that he had found a way to ensure her safety. Of course, after hearing that, she knew not to eat or talk on her cell phone while driving with her parents but after she got the hang of shifting gears, she knew juggling food or the phone—even both—would be a snap.

In thinking back on that moment, Chrys guessed that her father's decision was a similar one among parents across the country and throughout the ages: The best laid schemes of mom or pop can "oft go awry" and leave teen naught but a more perilous car for a more promising ride. She chuckled to herself. Uncle Jules had apparently turned her on to Robert Burns and Steinbeck more than she had realized. Grinning, she picked up the can of root beer from the holder, opened it and took a swig in the short lapse between downshifting and up-shifting in the turn onto McCabe.

Heading west into more rural territory, they passed streets or farms named in the same way her road had been, after the people who first settled there. But after a hundred years or more, most of those families no longer lived in the region. She tried to imagine what it would be like to have a street or landmark named after her. Surely, she wouldn't use her first name with its funny spelling but her surname, Stemmermann, was way too long to name anything, even people. How could all those letters fit on a street sign and still be seen by motorists? And could all those letters actually be squished onto the broad side of a barn without having to wrap a few around the side? She wished her great grandfather had done what a lot of immigrants do and Americanize their last name. One friend's last name, which was originally "Bakaris," was now "Baker." Why couldn't hers have been shortened at least to "Stemmer?" On second thought, though, that name along with the origin of her first, sounded much too botanical to be an improvement.

Up and over the interstate they breezed at five miles under the speed limit, past Reimer's Vegetable Stand, past Fulton's Dairy Farm, past Wilbur Lake, where it was too cold yet to swim. Still, going that slowly, Chrys appreciated the scenery and suddenly understood Sunday drivers. They crept along mile by mile, not to make her life miserable after all, but rather to take in the flowerbeds in that yard over there, the shimmering pond behind that one, or—she almost ran into the ditch—the garish red roof and purple shutters of that tasteless wonder. Iris in the back seat squeaked when

Chrys jerked the car back onto the road.

"It's okay, Iris," Chrys said. "I was just distracted."

"'Just distracted' doesn't cut it behind the wheel," Peri offered.

"Oh, I can't wait," she said gritting her teeth, "until next year when you start driving."

The few miles farther to Buckeye High School were filled with more sniping between Chrys and her brother. The ping-ponging between them got so fast and feisty that even William, who had no beef with Chrys, plus Iris, who rarely voiced her anxiety beyond an involuntary yelp, leaped into the circus ring of catty remarks and name-calling. William sided with Peri; Iris aligned herself with Chrys. Much to Chrys's relief she didn't have to take them all on. But with the four split up that way, the scene quickly escalated from a few shots fired over driving ability to a big-guns battle of the sexes.

Just when the comments bordered on vicious, Chrys spotted the rounded roof of Buckeye High's gym and administration building from the top of the hill. William, Peri and Iris got as quiet as a stone. And though Chrys's lips were primed with another verbal cannonball for Peri, she did too.

Down the slope the car glided and into the entrance. The parking lot was almost absent of cars since summer school hadn't begun yet, and Chrys didn't know whether to be worried or grateful that not many people would be milling about. If she or the others needed help or questions answered, they might not be able to find the right person; plus the absence of people would make their snooping around campus more conspicuous to the few custodians and office personnel who were there. Still, it would be easier than if the entire summer school staff and students were in session.

Chrys said nothing of these thoughts to the others. She

didn't want to raise another argument and have the camps divide over staying or leaving. They were there and so Chrys handed over the situation to fate. She swung into a parking space at the end of the building. Facing her were the many acres of mowed grass that surrounded it like a green apron and a few fifty-year-old maples planted so close to the school that their leaves threatened on this breezy day to scrape against the second-story windows.

The school, built in the 1950s out of tan brick and with the straightest of lines, except for a curved roof above the front section, was in the shape of a gigantic square. The idea behind the design, Chrys imagined, was to prevent the students from skipping class and wandering to the shopping center across the street. The architect must have been especially pleased with himself, and the school board especially pleased with the architect as the large courtyard in the center was also designed to keep the students contained. Dotted with picnic tables, it was where they were permitted to eat lunch outside. That is, if the weather permitted. Of course, in Ohio only four months out of the school year (September, October, April and May) offered that opportunity, minus two. Usually, October got too cold too fast to want to eat a cold sandwich outside and April drizzled a cold rain almost every day all day that squelched one's appetite altogether.

The land behind the school housed the soccer, baseball and football fields, six tennis courts and some outbuildings, including a couple storage sheds and the field house. It was this area that Chrys and the others headed for when they got out of the car. Peri said he would take on the field house and the football stadium. Before Chrys could object or agree, he was off and quickly disappeared around the backside of the complex. She surveyed the grounds then divvied up the sheds, which were several hundred yards away on the edge of the property, to the twins. She said she would scout the tennis courts and adjacent soccer field here on the south side of the school. William stood staring at her.

"What are you waiting for?" Chrys asked.

"What are we supposed to find again?"

"Anything that seems out of place or that has anything to do with Uncle Jules. A package, a letter, a book in a flippin' tool shed. Oh, I don't know—use Iris's sixth sense to help you sniff it out."

Iris, who had looked worried throughout the ride, now appeared so pleased she yanked at William's arm, and they marched off without glancing back.

Chrys covered the courts and soccer field in relative short order. Even after canvassing every foot of ground, walking along the edge of the tennis cage and looking under all the benches and into the trashcans, she came up empty-handed. She hung her head with disappointment but told herself that the others needed to check in before she should allow real sadness to overtake her. She looked up and around, expecting to see at least one of them finished and walking over. Several minutes passed with still no sign of any of them. Growing impatient, she moved into the shade of one of the maple trees and leaned against it. She peered into the nearby window of a classroom and suddenly curious, turned and walked to the front of the building. With a determination to comb over the entire area—inside as well as out—before giving up, she stepped gingerly to and then through the front door of the school.

Only once had she visited her uncle's classroom. Two years ago he had left his cell phone charging in his room the day before winter break and remembered it moments before dinner with her family. So her mother held dinner for forty minutes while he and Chrys drove back to get it.

As she now walked down that same hall toward his

room, an eerie feeling crept over her skin as though she were being watched. But no one was in the hall but her, and the people working in the offices seemed to pay no attention to her. After all, she was no cat-burglar, just a fifteen-year-old student who had left something important behind, like the last passionate note from her boyfriend, and without a clue that the custodians had already ravaged the lockers of their contents.

She rounded the back corner of the hall and hoping his classroom was unlocked, looked for #110. Surprisingly, the door was wide open. She slowed her pace and crossed to the same side of the hall as the room. She inched along as close to the lockers as she could without brushing against them. When she got to the door, she stopped. A heavy, haunting feeling across her shoulders like someone had slipped a lead poncho over her head. She contemplated turning back and running from the building. It was the same feeling she had when she and a friend cut through Sylvan Cemetery in Willow merely to make better time.

Again, she got a grip on herself and gave up the moment to fate. She snaked around the corner and peeked inside. The window was open and a swirling breeze blew her hair as if it were a ghost spiraling past her. Her spine prickled with both apprehension and excitement. She stepped into the threshold telling herself that even though this was hallowed ground, her presence was no desecration of it. Uncle Jules would want her there, she thought, if this place held the answer to his clue. A school not a school. Yes, this was a school, but her uncle had been much more than a teacher. For some of his students, this classroom had to have seemed like home.

Chrys took a couple steps inside and gazed above the blackboard where she remembered caricatures of famous authors. But in their place were posters citing grammatical don'ts: "Don't rely on spell check to catch all you're mistakes." Another said, "Make sure your subjects agrees with their verbs." At the other end of the blackboard was the tree her uncle had painted on the wall to match the one outside his room. He had brought the oak inside so everyone, not just those near the window, could enjoy it. With an art minor, a natural talent for landscape painting and a special friendship with dead authors who communed with nature and thanked broken shells on the beach for their godly messages, he had fashioned that tree with a detail that rivaled a good 35mm camera.

"Can I help you?" a booming voice rang out from the other end of the room.

Chrys nearly jumped out of her jeans. She spun around. A woman at the back of the room was kneeling in front of an open cabinet, the door of which concealed all but the lower part of her calves and feet. Chrys sputtered, "I ... I was just looking for—"but she had to stop there. What could she say she was looking for? Her dead uncle's treasure?

"You're not a Buckeye, are you?" the woman said standing. She was a forty-ish African American who rose taller than Chrys thought she would. She walked stiffly toward Chrys, flipped on the second set of lights next to the door, and eyed her closely. "No, I didn't think so." With a chuckle she said, "Now what's a teenager doing in the first few days of summer back in a school that's not your own?" She wiped her face with her hand then rested both hands on her hips.

"This was my uncle's room."

The woman's face immediately softened. "Mr. Miner was your uncle? Why, I knew your uncle for almost twenty years," she said with quiet respect. "We taught right across the hall from one other. Only he was literature and I was creative writing." She pointed through the open door to

63

#103 across the hall. "When I came on board here, green and scared of everything—the kids, parents, the principal—he just tucked me under his wing." She backed up and slipping into a student desk, motioned for Chrys to sit in the one next to her. "Which niece are you?"

"I'm Chrys. My mom's his sister."

"I'm Mrs. Carol. So what brings you here?"

"I guess I thought some of his things would still be here." Chrys now looked around the entire room to see that nothing of her uncle's belongings remained on the walls or shelves. "I guess I didn't realize that somebody else's things would be moved in."

"Sorry about that. But if it makes you feel any better, I simply jumped at the chance of living out my last ten years in the vibrations of this room. Plus, I had to make sure no one got rid of that tree. One day I heard a teacher in the lounge talk about how she was going to have it painted over and have shelves put in its place. Well, that was it. Seniority or not, I was in the principal's office demanding my right as your uncle's greatest admirer to preserve his memory at this school. Oh, it was just that one teacher really. And envy at that. Everyone else had enormous respect for your uncle and his many wonderful talents."

Wonderful talents? Chrys knew of her uncle's artistic ability and love of teaching, but that was it. "What talents do you mean?"

The woman rested her hand on Chrys's, gazed at her and sighed as though overwhelmed with the question. "Honey, I'd need all day to list them. But I'll tell you this. All the gifts he had whether it was plying paint or passages from a book, were used for one thing only—to push people into doing things they'd never imagined in their wildest dreams they could."

Chrys would have never guessed what Mrs. Carol just

said, but she also wasn't surprised with her answer. And though Mrs. Carol had been vague, Chrys understood her perfectly and smiled at her.

"Well, I'd better go," Chrys said rising from the chair. "My sister and brothers will be wondering where I am."

"I'm glad I got a chance to meet you, Chrys," she said rising.

"Me too."

Mrs. Carol placed her hand on Chrys's shoulder. "You come around anytime you feel like talking. I've got stories, lots of stories." She stopped and her eyes twinkled with both sadness and delight. "I'm sorry that's all I can offer you. His wife came and picked up the last few boxes a long time ago." But her eyes brightened and she held up her hand as a crossing guard would. "How do you spell your name?"

"C-h-r-y-s. Why?"

"Stay right there."

She moved through the aisle of desks to the back of the room and toward the set of tall cabinets. She opened one, brought out a stack of large papers and laid it on a nearby desk. Chrys saw it contained, among other things, Uncle Jules' posters. They must have been his legacy to her, Chrys thought. Near the bottom of the pile, Mrs. Carol pulled out a sheet of parchment paper. She gazed at it intently then walked to Chrys.

"He talked about his nieces and nephews all the time, so I don't know what in the world made me think this was meant for a student." She held out the stiff paper to Chrys.

Chrys's name was written at the top of the page in swirls of ornate calligraphy. It dawned on her that if she hadn't come inside, she might never have received this. As fast as that gloomy possibility had sneaked into her mind, though, Chrys chased it away, along with any chance for another. She was simply too thankful to have in her possession what

Uncle Jules had intended for her.

After he died, Aunt Lydia had given each of the children, except Chrys, a personalized message from Uncle Jules, on parchment like this one, found in his things. At times Chrys felt downhearted in not getting one, but she never felt unloved. She knew her uncle's gift to her would turn up eventually, even after Aunt Lydia had sifted through his things a dozen times.

Like the mementos for her siblings, this one contained lines of verse perfect for framing. Taking a deep breath, she read them out loud. "'For thy sweet love rememb'red such wealth brings/That then I scorn to change my state with kings.'" Tears welled up. "'From Sonnet 29,'" she said, pressing the paper to her. She nodded to Mrs. Carol and smiled wistfully. "Mine's from Shakespeare." Mrs. Carol nodded back, and Chrys rushed from the room.

Down the hall and around the corner she flew, her bones lightening and lightening until she imagined them as hollow as a bird's. She would open the front doors and soar above the ground. When she reached the entrance, the door suddenly flung open. Chrys thought it was confirmation of her supernatural powers, but the two boys barreled in and then Iris, every one of them looking exasperated and worried.

"Where the heck have you been?" Peri shouted. Then he stared at the paper she was clutching to her chest. "You found something?"

"Nothing," Chrys said bluntly. The twins went limp as they did a dejected u-turn in the doorway and plodded outside. Peri glared at her skeptically. But with a shove and her sharpest evil eye, she repeated "Nothing" and got him to head to the car with the twins. Following them tall and grinning, and looking at the paper again, she whispered, "No, it's everything."

CHAPTER 9

The walk to the car was deadly quiet. Chrys suspected the others were dealing with their failure to find anything that would further their quest. And though she wished she would have uncovered something too, she had a hard time pasting on as gloomy a face as they were wearing.

When they reached the car, Peri, William and Iris piled into the same seats as before and slumped into place without a second of quibbling. Before slipping behind the wheel, Chrys slid the paper into the pocket of the door and opened her mouth to break the excruciating silence just as Peri turned to her and beat her to the punch.

"So what *did* you find? Or were you planning on keeping us in perpetual suspense?"

She really didn't want to talk about it right now, believing that the wondrous spell she was under would break if she did. But Peri kept staring at her, and if she didn't say something, she knew he would dog her to death about it, completely killing the feeling of Uncle Jules' spirit moving within her.

"It's Uncle Jules' message to me, like the one you guys got," she said hoping it would be enough, then added in case it wasn't, "A couple lines from Shakespeare."

"Ooooh, yours is from Shakespeare. Aren't you special? Mine was from Walter Whitman, whoever he is."

"*Walt* Whitman," she said. "How do you not know that name? Whitman's an important poet. Really important."

"We never studied him."

"Then why didn't you look him up?"

Peri seemed slighted and shifted in his seat. "What does yours say? Let's see it."

She didn't want his paws to touch the paper and she certainly wasn't going to read it aloud and risk bursting into tears. She thought for a moment. "It says that as long as a person is loved he shouldn't want to trade his life, even with a king's." She blinked away tears that were blurring the road before her. "Satisfied?"

"Gee, I didn't understand mine," William said.

"Neither did I," Iris added.

Peri turned his face toward the window.

"You didn't get yours either, did you Peri?" Chrys said. She blew hot air onto her fingernails and polished them on her shirtfront. "Well, I guess that proves who the real brains are." She swung her head around. "William, Iris, don't worry. I'll get us through this. Ghost-reader, literary-reader extraordinaire, at your service." And she smiled broadly.

"You better watch it," Peri said, "or your head's gonna swell up so big that the only place you'll feel at home is next to the fat lady in a sideshow." He erupted into deep laughter that quickly infected William and even enticed Iris to giggle.

Chrys, her face hot with rage, clicked on the radio loud enough to stifle any further conversation between them. When Peri had played the joke for all it was worth and the laughter subsided, she turned her thoughts to the mission that seemed to have reached a dead end.

When the music ended and a commercial came on, William asked, "So what do we do now?" He rubbed his hands together. "There's a treasure out there to find."

Chrys glanced at him through the rearview mirror. "*We* aren't going to do anything. And really, you can stop sounding like some greedy little fool."

William lowered his head. "Just trying to help," he murmured.

"What do you mean, '*we* aren't going to do anything?'" Peri said his voice rising. "You give us that holier-than-thou attitude and then bail out? Give me a pin, somebody, so I can pop that beach ball perched on top of her shoulders!"

The rest of the ride home was one of more laughter from the boys and blaring music. When they finally quieted, William claimed a side ache and starvation, so he opened the cooler beside him and handed out the sandwiches and sodas. Chrys refused hers. After another ten minutes they rolled into the driveway and simultaneously poured from the car. Chrys shot ahead of them and with her nose to the heavens marched to and through the house, up the stairs and into her room without saying a word or making eye contact with any of them. At her bedroom door she flicked her hair back with a snap of her head and slammed the door shut.

A minute later she heard William and Peri clomping up the stairs. Chrys pressed her ear to the door.

"Sure it was funny," William said, "but why'd you have to be so mean? Now what are we going to do?"

"We ... don't ... need ... her," Peri said as though purposely projecting the words through her door.

"Oh yes we do," Iris's small voice said. "I can feel it."

"Good girl, Iris," Chrys whispered.

Their conversation then subsided and the house remained quieter than usual until her parents came home at five-thirty. Iris watched TV downstairs then played with her dolls in her room. Late in the afternoon Chrys heard Peri and William strike up a game of one-on-one basketball below her window. Occasionally, one of them, Peri probably, beaned the side of the house where her room was. No matter how annoying the sound was, she never once screamed out the window. No, she hoped he'd sail the ball through her window and then catch the devil for it. He would have to clean up the broken glass, pay for the window, and help her father replace it—a fitting sight to see him quailing on a ladder for the damage he had done to her earlier.

Tuning out the dribbling, the pings against the backboard, and the whooshes—even the slams against the house—she pulled a book from a shelf. It was the collected works of Shakespeare that Uncle Jules had given to her two years ago for her thirteenth birthday. It was over a hundred years old and its leather cover was ornately tooled in three colors. She debated about reading from it. She knew using it over and over again would spoil its mint condition. But more importantly, it didn't have the added features of the other copy he gave her when he had stopped teaching—a plainer copy but containing his notes in the margins. She replaced the older book and slid out the newer one, the one she had picked up the night of Uncle Jules' visitation and read from *Romeo and Juliet*. Whenever she opened that book, she imagined she somehow entered her uncle's head as well as Shakespeare's. Often she pictured him in front of the classroom, that book laid open in his hands, imparting wisdom or insight. Turning through the pages, she spotted "Sonnet 29." Carefully, she read through it to put the quote he had given her in context. The poem's language and message were even more beautiful than she could have imagined.

She spent the rest of the day trying to rewrite the poem with her calligraphy felt pens well enough to frame it and hang it next to the lines Uncle Jules had rendered. Several times the basketball bouncing off the house made her mess up, and though she had to start again, she called Peri "a child" under her breath and so kept herself calm. By the time she heard her mother drive in, Chrys had just finished

Shakespeare's name at the bottom and grinned at her accomplishment. She placed it next to her uncle's. Tomorrow she would go into Willow and buy two frames.

The boys stopped playing long enough for their mother to pull her car into the garage, collect her things, and push the button to lower the garage door when she got to the house. Chrys, hearing her mother call out for the girls to help with dinner, wondered whether Gothic slime would again be an ingredient.

Chrys met up with Iris in the kitchen but gave her the cold shoulder even when they stood together at the kitchen sink peeling potatoes. A couple times Iris looked as though she were about to speak but glanced at their mother and then didn't. The potatoes were on the stove and the chicken in the oven when her mother scooped up her keys and purse.

"Where're you going?" Chrys asked.

"Drymon's Market. We're out of lettuce."

"I can go for it."

"Thanks Sweetie, but by the time you bike there and back, everything else will be done. You two can work on the rest of the salad while I'm gone." She kissed Chrys and Iris on the tops of their heads and zipped out the back door.

Chrys went to the refrigerator and piled in her arms a head of red cabbage, a sweet onion, and a cucumber from the vegetable bin. After rolling them onto the kitchen counter next to the sink, she pointed to the bowl of tomatoes on the table.

"Get a couple of those, will you?" she said to Iris.

Iris obeyed and while washing them said, "Sorry about today."

"It's all right. Besides, you didn't start it."

"Chrys, you're not really going to bail out, are you?" Iris said with a wrinkled forehead.

"I don't know," Chrys said to appease Iris, though she had no intention of changing her mind.

By the time her mother returned, she and Iris had peeled and sliced the veggies for the salad, but her mother looked hardly pleased when she came through the door. As a matter of fact, she looked positively crazed when she locked her eyes on Chrys.

"What's wrong?" Chrys asked.

Her mother slammed her keys on the counter. "You drove the Jetta by yourself?"

Chrys was so taken off guard as to how her mother could possibly know that her tongue tied into a Celtic knot she thought she might never undo. Was her mother a clairvoyant who had managed to hide her talent for fifteen years? Chrys looked at her with eyes popping and that knot in her tongue tightening by the second.

"Just admit it. I know you did."

Finally, Chrys choked out, "How?"

"I didn't take my car. I took the Jetta and happened to notice the sticker on the windshield from the oil change three days ago. The gas station's only three miles from here and that car hasn't been driven anywhere since. Now suddenly there's more than *twenty* miles on it than should be. How could you do such a dangerous thing? And where did you go that we couldn't have gone together?"

"I ... I promise, I stayed on back roads the whole time and drove way under the speed limit."

"That doesn't matter. It's the law. And if you would have gotten stopped for how young you look, well, I can't even imagine what would have happened with your permit or your permanent license, not to mention how far into outer space our insurance would have sky-rocketed. You took that kind of risk simply for the fun of driving by yourself?"

Chrys debated telling her mother about the mission but based on the anger in her voice, she decided the best tack was to look sheepish and shrug her shoulders. Her mother sighed with exhaustion and thorough frustration at the same time. She handed Chrys the lettuce with a stern look that said the rest of dinner and setting the table was her job. "I can't talk to you about this anymore right now," she said heading toward the kitchen door. "Besides, your father ought to be part of this conversation too—as well as what punishment you're to get."

A chill ran up Chrys's spine, giving her a splitting pain through the top of her skull that rivaled an ice cream headache. Iris seemed afraid to look at her, but did squeak out another "Sorry." This time Chrys didn't reply. She was too busy running through the possibilities of her punishment. Would her parents beat her? Of course not. But she almost wished that corporal punishment was an option. Stinging but swift, it would put no chink in her mission. Would they sell the car? Take away her music? Or ground her for the rest of the summer when it had only just begun? That would be the worst, the one impossible to swallow. If that turned out to be her parents' choice, she resolved somehow to convince her mother of Uncle Jules' mission for her and so get her mother to adjust the penalty.

Through the kitchen window she saw her father's car round the back of the house. When he got out, he said "Hey" to the boys, asked who was ahead and promised the winner a game after dinner. Then he told them to wrap up the game and wash up. Chrys slipped into the living room and lay down on the couch with the hope that her father would walk by without seeing her. She breathed a sigh of relief when he did. Much more time then passed for her father simply to change clothes and trot downstairs for his twenty-minute read of the daily newspaper before dinner.

Eventually, he and her mother came down together and separated at the bottom of the stairs. Her mother disappeared into the kitchen; her father headed to the den.

When they all assembled around the dinner table, Chrys prepared herself for the hammer blow to her life. As big as her mistake was, her parents would surely break their rule about saving unpleasantries until after dinner and digestion. Surprisingly, they said nothing of the incident over the garlicky roast chicken, mashed potatoes, and tossed salad. Chrys spent much of the time staring at one of her favorite meals—no gruesome slime here—and trying to choke down enough of it not to draw even more attention to herself, especially from William and Peri, who she believed knew nothing about the scene with her mother in the kitchen. Iris knew not to tattle if she hoped to continue to have a sister to talk to.

Finally, the day and a half it seemed to take to finish dinner was over. The boys had the job of clean-up so they picked up all the plates, put the glasses and silverware on a tray, and headed into the kitchen. Iris glanced at Chrys with a look of sympathy in her large eyes and then slipped away after her mother suggested she go play with Jenny, a friend who lived a few doors away.

Her mother led Chrys into the den where her father had also gravitated. He was sitting in one of a pair of leather chairs that sat opposite a couch. He motioned for Chrys to take the loveseat, her mother to sit in the companion leather chair. Oh great, Chrys thought, a solid front. At times in the past, her mother had parked next to her on the couch and counseled her shoulder to shoulder. But this time Chrys was facing a firing squad. If she hadn't believed her parents would charge her with sounding flippant, she would have asked for a blindfold.

Her father looked pensive as he rubbed his hands

together. "Chrys, do you understand the gravity of what you did? Do you know what awful things might have happened to you?"

"I do now. I just wasn't thinking at the time. Driving the car was the only choice."

"To do what?" her mother asked.

Chrys hung her head. "To get to Uncle Jules' school."

Her mother looked at her father and then back to her. "Why would you go there? It's been months since he quit teaching."

"I told you before. Uncle Jules visited me."

Her mother looked as though she might come over and put her arms around Chrys, but her father placed his hand on her knee, stopping her from getting up.

"Chrys, I understand you're hurting," her mother said in that same controlled voice she used in talking to the residents of New Life Habitat. "We all are. And I know you want to find a way to hang onto him, but breaking the law just isn't the right way to accomplish that."

She peered intently at her mother. "But he said we had to find 'a school that's not a school.'"

"Did he write that to you?"

"No, he said it to me the night of his funeral. His ghost came into my room and he gave me a mission to solve—'for the benefit of the living.' So what do you think he meant?"

Her mother looked at Chrys as though she had been handed papers to commit her eldest daughter to a mental institution. She straightened herself in the chair, cleared her throat and played with a button on her blouse. As though she was talking to a wounded animal she said, "I don't know, Chrys. Maybe he meant 'life.'"

She teared up and Chrys knew her mother hadn't believed a word she'd told her about Uncle Jules. Chrys loved her mother and she wanted to make her understand, especially since her mother and Uncle Jules were so close, but Chrys couldn't make the same mistake again and risk a straitjacket as her school attire in the fall.

After a visual exchange between her mother and father and then a nod from her father, her mother seemed to recover. With a more logical tone and drier eyes she said, "Maybe, Chrys, it's the school of experience you're looking for. Your uncle always told you to love life as much as you love books."

Suddenly her father's eyes grew sharp. "Chrys, you said *we*. '*We* had to find a school not a school.' Who else was involved in this?"

"Oh my God," her mother said wringing her hands. "Tell me you didn't have one of the other children with you!"

"No..." Chrys said and noticed her mother's face relaxed some, but Chrys couldn't carry the untruth. "All of us went."

Her mother went limp in the chair and looked as though she might faint. Her father slid to the front of his seat, put his elbows on his knees and cupped his jaw in his hands.

"This is worse than we could have imagined. It's one thing to violate our trust in taking the car; it's another to endanger the lives of three other people." He ran his hands over his face and through his hair. As his lips parted to speak, there was a knock on the partially closed door and then it swung open. Peri poked in his head.

"How about that game, Dad?"

"Peri, step in here. And close the door behind you." Peri did as he was told. "You're fourteen years old. I hold you partly responsible for what happened today."

Peri's eyes burned at Chrys. "For *what* that happened today?"

"For agreeing to ride with Chrys and allowing the twins

76

to go with you to Buckeye High." Before Peri could create any kind of defense, their father looked at Chrys and slowly said, "You. young lady, are grounded for double what your mother and I had agreed on. That means for the next two weeks no driving the car or travel of any kind, except for errands; no socializing and no use of the computer. Plan on extra chores around here to fill some of your time."

Chrys nodded without smiling, but inside her head she was screaming with joy and jumping up and down. Her life and her mission wasn't over after all. Then their father cleared his throat and interrupted her internal dance.

"One more thing. If you take the car a second time without your mother or me, you won't have a car to do it a third." He then turned to Peri who had opened his mouth, apparently ready to offer something lame to plead his case. Their father held up his hand to silence him. "And to contemplate *your* choices, you get a week of the same."

CHAPTER 10

Now it was Peri's turn to give Chrys the silent treatment and he did so for the remainder of that evening. William, as though part of Peri's army, also kept his distance from her. But she was unfazed by their childishness. Even if a time came when she was truly desperate for someone to talk to, there was always Iris. Chrys guessed, though, that not much time would pass before her big-mouth brother would not be able to keep the lid on his anger and so to avoid bursting at the seams he would have to spout his tirade about her being the "informant." At that point she could spout "Touché!" and shut her voice and bedroom door to him.

She wondered, though, if she could keep her lips sealed for two solid weeks if Peri should lose his cool sooner rather than later. She wished that her two friends were available to call—after all, Chrys's parents hadn't prohibited her from talking to others, just meeting up with them. But one friend was working full time at the drugstore in Willow and wasn't allowed personal calls, and the other had flown out the day after school ended on a month-long vacation to Europe with her family. Chrys hadn't felt jealous at the time, though Janice glowed about it, but now she was beginning to. Why couldn't her parents have planned such a trip? Her worries at the moment would be over, would be non-existent as she stood under the Eiffel Tower or in the Coliseum. Though her parents had wished they could take such an educational trip, their nest egg was sitting in a college savings account.

They promised Chrys that by the time she graduated, if she worked each summer and they all cut back on some things, there would be enough money for a special trip, maybe to San Francisco for a week. Upon hearing what amounted to a three-year-plan, Chrys had felt absolutely despondent, but after Uncle Jules' visitation and the mission he put her on, she laid the matter to rest. Now, the emptiness of her life and the fullness of her friend's in Europe turned her still greener with envy.

She selected the blended music of Bond and turned the sound low—like dimming the lights, so the music wouldn't fill the room and her head but set the mood and let her think. Like the faint brush of leaves against a window, it would merely hold in memory the world outside her room. She read through Shakespeare's Sonnet 29 that she had transcribed and then read again the two isolated lines of it from Uncle Jules. Was his mission for them just a trick? She couldn't help questioning how far she had gone and what sacrifices and risks she had taken in seeking the "treasure." What if all this was a wild goose chase to keep her and the others busy over the summer or worse, was some elaborate joke. She recalled some of his April Fools pranks and the year he gave her a birthday present of a necklace with huge orange rhinestones that not even her grandmother would have worn, beyond masquerading as Wilma Flintstone on Halloween, that is. Chrys had tried her best to look appreciative, but her mouth gaped and when she sputtered, "Thank you," he screamed, "Gotcha!" He swung his arm from around his back and produced another present. In it was a dainty Tiffany heart pendant and chain. She wasn't a fan of dainty jewelry but because Uncle Jules had given it to her, she cried when she saw it and then they both had a glorious laugh over her reaction to the fake gift. Her mother, an obsessive-compulsive videographer, had recorded the whole scene so Chrys's naivety could be forever relived for every cousin, aunt, and grandparent. So was Uncle Jules' mission for her and the others just another way for him to continue his fun, only this time make her appear retarded in the end, not only to her family but to the entire cosmos of souls?

Her brain was throbbing by this time, and seeing the clock display the beginning of another day, she decided midnight was a respectable hour for a teen to hit the sack. Going to bed too early, even though it would have been easy to doze off that night, would have sent a dangerous signal of her depression to Peri, who'd have more fuel to use against her whenever he decided to reactivate his vocal cords.

When she awoke the following morning, she lazed so long between the sheets that she began to fret that she would develop bedsores if she lingered any longer. So she rolled out of bed, dressed and plodded down the stairs like a tortoise in slow motion. She had two weeks to kill—she might as well drag everything out as long as possible, especially the extra chores awaiting her. She could see it now—a plentiful list of them on the refrigerator, each requiring hours to complete. As she swung open the kitchen door, she was not disappointed, at least not in her prophecy. She was disappointed, however, in her parents' steadfastness that produced a list far longer than she had envisioned. And they had to print out the list in red and eighteen point font, to boot! Chrys remembered her English teacher saying that any writing assignment with a font other than black or bigger than twelve points looked like a fifth grader's paper. She looked at their list for Peri. Oh well, she thought, at least it looked like a ten-year-old was hollering orders at him too.

Quickly, she read through the list, which wasn't numbered and so gave her the opportunity to do the jobs as the spirit moved her. Included on the list were chores like de-scaling the two showers upstairs and the one in the basement, cleaning the baseboards of the entire house, and wiping out all the drawers and cupboards of the kitchen and bathrooms. Although she hated those jobs, she grinned in reading Peri's, which included cleaning out the gutters. She was glad that in recent years he didn't speak about his fears to his parents. A macho thing, she gathered. But she had detected more than once how he stayed away from high rides at amusement parks and positively paled in climbing a ladder. So she rejoiced that her chores, though as tedious as his, kept her feet—not his—on the ground.

At five-thirty on the third day of her imprisonment, she was inside the basement shower, soaked all over, the skin on her feet and hands wrinkled like an elephant's backside. Just as she was praising herself for picking the perfect time to clean the shower, right when her mother would have come home and seen her toiling away, the phone rang. Peri was outside on the ladder; the twins were at their friends'. Chrys let the phone ring the five times to let the answering machine pick it up. She stopped scrubbing, though, when she heard her mother's voice repeating louder and louder for someone to answer. Dripping, Chrys jumped out of the shower and scooted up the slick wooden stairs as gingerly as she could without breaking her neck.

"Hello?" she said.

"Chrys?"

"I'm dripping on the floor," Chrys said.

"Why? What are you doing?"

"Cleaning the shower."

"But why would you be dripping?"

"I put on my bathing suit to get a shower too. Why did you call?"

"I need you to go to Drymon's and pick up some of their smoked ribs for dinner. I'm running late. Throw some bakers in the oven and some broccoli in the microwave."

"Sure," Chrys said and grinned, "be glad to." She smiled wider. It was the only chance she had in days to get out of a wet, tiring chore and a dry, boring house. She almost ruined it for herself, though, by starting to yell "Yippee" before she hung up. She covered with an immediate apology for sneezing into the phone.

Within five minutes she had dressed and hauled her bike from the garage. Peri still wasn't speaking to her but he did turn around from the ladder and sneer at her as if to ask where in the heck she was going. Getting on her bike, she veiled her eyes and pointed her nose to the clouds as if to say it was none of his business—better still, with a flick of her hair she dared him to speak anything at all—then rode off.

Unlike all the other times when she ran errands at break-neck speed to get them over with or beat it to Drymon's before they closed at eight, she now took her time. Only three days had elapsed since she had been confined to the house; still, she felt as if she hadn't seen these things in years: the well-kept houses along McCabe with their vegetable gardens, the smell of freshly mown hay, or the creaking and clanking sound of a swing set. The feeling was like the way navel oranges taste in the fall after months of nothing but frozen concentrate. Denied fruit, she thought, was always sweeter.

She turned off McCabe onto Beyer, a dirt road with a washboard surface, the usual shortcut in dry weather. She slowed her peddling even more with the bumpy ride and so saved her kidneys from trauma. As when she was very little, she opened her mouth and vocalized a long "ahhhh" that transformed into the sound of a machine gun. About halfway down this dirt road, she stopped and dismounted in order to walk her bike through a park-like piece of property, filled with tall oaks, pines and flowering dogwoods. She wondered why it didn't have a house on it but she couldn't recall ever seeing a "For Sale" sign posted. Maybe it belonged to one of the houses on either side, the owner believing that distance created better neighbors. But these lots were already large, a couple acres at least. Oh well, she thought, all the better for her to have this hypotenuse of a shortcut.

Walking her bike through the trees, she remembered that sense of Sunday drivers. She took a deep breath as though the stale air in her lungs from being cooped up for days was being replaced with the sweet, pure air that gives sheets dried outdoors that wonderful smell. She stopped once to pluck a bloom from a pink dogwood. After running her fingers along the velvety petals, she worked the stem under the hair tie holding her ponytail. She was still smiling when she finally reached the main road. Mounting her bike, she could see the front porch of Drymon's Market a quarter of a mile ahead.

This mom-and-pop store had originally been a two-story residence, the grandest of Loyal Oak's beginnings. Home to the founder of the town, it was much more than the "five, four and a door" houses so popular in row-type subdivisions. This one had a wide, wrap-around porch with a half dozen rocking chairs, high-pitched roofs with cupolas, and shutters with decorative cut-outs on all the windows. From old photographs over its one hundred and twenty-five year history, Chrys knew the house possessed several add-ons to the original building, giving it a sense of mystery as though it were the Winchester Mansion. Try as she might, however, as many times as she had walked around that place, she had never seen anything unusual like stairs going nowhere. Still, the multiple layers of paint peeling as though the house had undergone a bad sunburn, its sagging porch that made it look tired, and the wooden columns with ants moving in and out of their cracks, made her question why the owners didn't try to restore such a prominent landmark of the past. As a little girl she often dreamed of owning the house and fixing it up for her and her husband, their eight children that the house could well support, and the ghosts that surely were residing there.

She rolled her front wheel into the bike rack in Drymon's small parking lot. Then two at a time, she climbed the weather-beaten steps to the porch and swung open the screen door. Mrs. Drymon, who was behind the counter, waved to her when she stepped in, offered her best to the rest of the family and asked Chrys what she'd come for. Chrys said she'd pass her wishes on to her mother and asked for three pounds of ribs. Nodding, Mrs. Drymon disappeared into a back room.

Suddenly, the screen door behind Chrys creaked open and a voice said, "Hey, Chrysler! I *thought* that was your bike outside."

It was Jack. She could feel her neck and face quickly grow hot, like a thermometer placed under scalding water. But before she could spin around and spew at him the fire on the tip of her tongue, he spoke again.

"Sorry, Chrys, force of habit. I was just surprised to find you here." His feet shuffled and his voice hemmed and hawed. "I thought you were grounded."

She could feel the blood drain from her face, move down, and pool in her feet. Her knees wobbled and she stammered, "How did you know I was grounded?" But before he could answer, she said, "Peri."

"No, actually, it was William. I ran into him earlier. I've been fixing the fence at my grandmother's house for extra money, and she lives on the same road where William and Iris were playing." He looked down at the floor. His feet moved slightly back and forth, and he seemed to be studying them.

"So what are you doing here?" she said. "There's a Kroger a block from your house."

"Gram wanted a few things before I headed home. So ... were you allowed out of the house?" He lifted his head and his large brown eyes twinkled at her. "Or did you escape?"

"Mom's getting home late, so she asked me to make dinner with Drymon's ribs."

She sniffed the air. "They're the best, better than Adam's Rib in Willow."

"I'll tell my mom to try them."

"Ooooo ... are you just stalling until the rest of the gang shows up?"

"Nobody else is coming. Honest."

"Then why are you talking to me?" Vague delight swept through her, but after all the agony he had caused, she wanted to see him squirm.

"You haven't shown up in town lately. And when you stopped coming to the library ..."

"Ahhh, you missed making fun of me."

"Oh, that Chrysler thing's over. Honest. It was that doofus, Chuckie, not me. But you've got to admit that the spelling makes a guy wonder." And he raised his eyebrows as though asking her to explain.

Chrys laughed. "Chuckie Doofus, huh? I like that. That's even funnier than his real name, Chuckie Duffy."

While they laughed over it, Mrs. Drymon returned with a large tray of ribs. She pulled out a three-foot length of white butcher paper, wrapped the meat tightly and secured the bundle with masking tape. She put the package in a plastic bag and handing the handles of it to Chrys, said it would be twenty-four dollars. Chrys gave her a twenty and a five, grabbed a candy bar from the shelf beneath the counter and brandished it so that Mrs. Drymon put the dollar back into the register.

In the meantime Jack had picked up a hand basket and wandered off between the aisles of canned goods. Chrys met up with him between the dried pasta and the canned meats.

Looking up at the clock, she said, "I've got to get going."

"Maybe we can talk again sometime?"

"While I'm grounded, I can't use the computer. And the house phone with extensions everywhere is definitely a no-no."

"Then I'll call your cell," he said, hooking his little finger around hers.

"Okay," she said with a timidity she didn't know she possessed. Yet she let his touch linger for a few seconds before she pulled away and said, "I'll get a pen."

When Chrys got to the counter, Mrs. Drymon handed her the pen she kept on the counter with a knowing grin. Chrys smiled with embarrassment, walked back to Jack, and wrote her number on the label of a tuna can in his basket. They exchanged another glance while he again touched her hand. Chrys, feeling a blanket's warmth move up and over her, again noted the time and sped out of the store.

Outside, her feet refused to land on the steps and the lightning speed with which she peddled home made her feel as though her lungs were malfunctioning. Over and over again, she let the bike coast while she tried to catch her breath. Then she pumped again furiously to expend that wild burst of energy and feel the air cool her hot skin. Her heart was pounding in her ears when she zoomed into the driveway, but she was hard pressed to know how much she should blame the frantic fifteen-minute ride for her state or Jack's words and touch.

Putting up her bike, she reminded herself that she had not liked a boy since third grade for a reason—all males were immature. She had convinced herself that only in college would she find someone she could talk to, someone she could trust. Never in her most outlandish dreams did she think Jack, of all people, could be that someone. They hadn't really talked and she surely had no reason to trust him, yet she couldn't get him out of her mind. His dark hair, almost black, and his soft brown eyes glinting at her loomed in her mind like a gigantic portrait on a wall. He was almost six feet she guessed, and she envisioned leaning on him and resting her head in that depression under his broad shoulder.

At the back door she posed in front of the mirror of the glass, fluttered her eyes, and swept her hair across her cheek. She had pursed her lips and fluffed her hair when a voice inside her head asked whether her memory of what had happened with Jack was faulty. Was he merely playing another joke at her expense that he would go back and tell to the other guys? Oh, the laugh they'd get out of this one! The voice cautioned her to swallow the incident and take her heart plastered on her sleeve like a Girl Scout badge and stow it. She ran her hand over her face and as she did, her expression turned deadpan. She took a deep calming breath, stepped inside, and swung the package of ribs onto the counter with a thud as though it were a reeled-in fish.

She was glad to have something to accomplish; it would keep her mind occupied. So she scrubbed the potatoes and ran the aluminum spikes through them to cut the baking time in half. By seven o'clock when her mother walked through the door, the potatoes were soft inside with crunchy skins, the broccoli crisp-tender and laced with melted cheddar cheese, and the table set. Her mother looked relieved but exhausted. She gave Chrys a wink and a gentle pinch on the cheek as thank you.

Dinner was relatively quiet with Peri still not speaking to Chrys and actually not saying much to anyone else except to answer questions with as few words as possible. Chrys guessed that when Peri found out she was sent on the errand instead of him, he decided to punish his parents with silence as well. Their mother didn't seem to mind not talking and at one point apologized for a rough day of so many words with patients that she now had none for the family. After all the times her mother had been tongue-worn, Chrys could still not understand the idea of being wordless, of looking at that blackboard in her mind and not seeing words or sentences automatically appear on it. Then her heart leapt with the thought of that moment with Jack, and she realized that in those seconds she had been speechless too.

After dinner Chrys waited what time seemed sufficient for her mother to regain her vocabulary and approached her in the den, where she was reading. Her father was outside playing b-ball with the boys; Iris was watching TV in the kitchen and drawing pictures of horses.

Chrys stole into the room quietly and sat down next to her mother on the couch. "Sorry you had a bad day."

Her mother patted Chrys's arm. "I'm better. Your having dinner ready really helped."

"No problem," Chrys said and shifting in the seat, decided she could safely change the subject. "I want to ask you a question. I've been thinking a long time about something, something that really bothers me."

Her mother turned more toward her. "What is it, Chrys?"

"Well, I don't mean to upset you. But this is a pretty big deal."

"Not knowing what it is, I can't say I won't be upset, but if *you* are, then we need to talk about it."

Chrys cringed then said as gently as she could, "I want to change my name—legally."

Instantly, the room was so quiet that Chrys imagined

the moment to be the split second of utter stillness before a nuclear blast. Her mother looked as if she'd been hit by one. Then she tried to recover and look calm, but the lines on her forehead gave her away.

"Why would you want to do that?" she said. "And change it to what?"

Chrys immediately tried to soothe her mother's ruffled love of flowers. "I don't want to change it completely, like for a totally different name. I just want to change the spelling. It's so weird-looking, people are always making fun of it or stumbling over the pronunciation."

"Oh," her mother said and seemed to struggle to find more words to go with it. "I don't know, Sweetie. Your names mean so much to me. You're going to have to give me some time to think about *this*." That last word, pronounced as if dirty, opened the floodgates of her emotion. She began to sob, as Chrys had never seen her do. Coming in huge heaves, her crying seemed like a river crashing down from a mountain whose origin was unknown and possibly unstoppable. Chrys put her arms around her and said, "Sorry," so many times that she thought she would use up that word for the rest of her life. And the more she said it, the more guilt swelled in her throat, so much so that she became certain that any other word attempted would choke her to death.

After a minute her mother collected herself enough to take normal breaths, sit back, and say, "Things were so much better when Julius was alive."

"But he is still with us..." Chrys whispered and she hugged her again—it was all she could think of doing.

Her mother suddenly caught herself, pulled back and looked at Chrys.

"Honey, your uncle is gone. You need to face that."

"But I saw him. I talked with him. He sent me on a

mission."

Worry etched deep wrinkles into her mother's face. "What kind of 'mission'?"

Chrys hesitated. "To find a treasure."

Her mother put her hand to her mouth. "Oh my word. Oh Chrys..."

"I'm not crazy. He really did visit me."

"A dream, Honey. It was just a dream."

"He was no dream," Chrys said sternly.

Her mother sighed and stared out the window with even deeper worry lines in her forehead. "Things were ever so much better when he was alive...."

Chrys didn't know whether to feel sorry for her mother or indignant about her mother's lack of belief. But she did know that she would not bring up the subject again and risk looking not half, but completely delusional. She rose and left the room wondering what exactly the "things" were that her mother believed were so much better before Uncle Jules died. She knew her mother automatically meant the sheer enjoyment of having him around, but now her mother's reaction implied so much more....

CHAPTER 11

Chrys walked upstairs deliberating about knocking on Peri's door and persuading him to bury his enormous hatchet. By the time she got to his door, she was convinced that the root cause of their mother's distress was his constant sarcasm and his silence. It couldn't be Chrys. She had simply affirmed her love and loyalty for her uncle and requested changing her name. Still, she guessed that mentioning it must have been a small thorn in her mother's side. But, it wasn't as though she said she despised her name and wanted a totally different one or picked up the papers at the courthouse and shoved them, all filled out, under her mother's nose.

With her fist poised in front of Peri's door, she debated about how talking to him might change her jockeying position among the four. As the oldest she didn't want to seem weak, especially to the twins, who would know about her "pleading" with Peri ten seconds after she left his room.

She opted to wait.

The rest of that evening and the remainder of that first week of captivity was one of utter boredom, more bathroom labor, and sore knees from washing the baseboards. She had first tried using the vacuum with the brush attachment but soon discovered that in the kitchen and dining room the baseboards weren't layered merely with dust but also with oily dirt as clingy as her friend's boyfriend and almost as greasy. As much as she liked the fresh French fries her mother occasionally made and the fondue nights with everyone's own colored fork, Chrys decided she'd talk to her mother about eliminating those foods for the greater cholesterol health of everyone.

In addition to the drudgery of that week, what also bothered her was the twins' apparent loss of interest in Uncle Jules' mission. Neither one had mentioned it after William whined about how Chrys ruined his chances for wealth, and she responded by calling him a subterranean money grubber. As for Peri? Who the heck knew what flotsam was floating in his head? But what was even more bothersome over those days—outright disturbing at times— was her not hearing from Jack.

She felt sure that he would call her the very next day. But when several days passed and *nothing*, she started to wonder whether she had been made the butt of still another joke. So by the end of that third day she was agonizing over what Jack probably shared with his cronies: how she smiled shyly at him, let him touch her hand and then wrote down her phone number for him. Ugh. Wiping the baseboard with greater vigor, she was certain that at that very moment she was the laughing stock of Willow. Well, if that's the way Mr. Jack Pitcher wanted to play, throwing such a curve, then she would try her best to smack it out of the park and make him look the fool. But exactly how she was going to accomplish that task escaped her when Peri popped his head into the kitchen and caught her on her knees of servitude on the tile floor.

"I'm free and I'm off to Willow," he said smugly.

Not looking around and wringing her sponge, she said, "You're free but you're still an unfeeling jerk."

"Oh Big Flower, tell me more." And the door slammed behind him.

Chrys stopped and a hurt rose in her that could have

stopped her heart. She rubbed her eyes to send them back where they came from. How dare Peri use Uncle Jules's nickname against her. She thought Peri understood that anything connected to Uncle Jules was sacred ground. Then she remembered her mother's last words from the night before. She didn't mean that "things" were better when Uncle Jules was alive; she meant that *the kids* were. Chrys's eyes welled up again, but she furiously scrubbed a section of baseboard to make them go away before they spilled over and raced down her face.

Two hours later she had finished chores for the day and was stepping out of the shower when her cell phone chirped, signally a text message. She wrapped the towel snugly around her, dashed to her room, and picked up her phone. She hesitated in looking at the caller. If it wasn't Jack, she'd be anguished. Yet if it was, she didn't want to find out that he along with her brother was a bona fide fathead. She took a deep breath and with hope tingling in her fingertips, she opened the message.

"Hey. Sorry it's been so long but I lost phone use. How r u doing?"

She texted him back. "Lol How'd that happen?"

"My mom got the phone bill. I went over by 32 bucks."

"Ouch."

"Yeah, I've got to pay her back w/the money I earn at Gram's."

"Ouch x 2."

"You got 1 more wk, huh? So why did u get grounded?"

Chrys hesitated again. She debated whether to give out such sensitive information that would only add another story to his repertoire to share with the goons he called friends.

"U still there?" he wrote.

"I drove the car all by myself. Worse—Peri and the twins were with me. My parents nearly stroked, said if I do it again they'll sell the car."

"Triple ouch. Why'd u do it?"

Chrys panicked at what she could say to be truthful and yet not go into detail about the mission they were on. Although she was glowing with good feelings about Jack, she couldn't trust him totally, even if he had opened up about his being de-phoned. "We drove out to Buckeye High, my uncle's school. We were looking for something."

"Oh. Yeah. Sorry about your uncle. I heard u were really close. So did u find what u went 4?"

"Lines from a poem he meant to give me before he died. I'm going to buy a frame for it as soon as I'm released from prison."

"I'd like to go with u. I've thought a lot about u since our day at D's Mkt."

Chrys's heart leaped from her chest and danced about the room. Like an old black and white movie she had seen once, she pictured herself dancing up the walls and on the ceiling.

Our day. She stared at the words so long that he wrote again.

"Did I say something wrong?"

"No. And sure, u can come w/me."

"Great. Let's see, next Thurs. at 3 ok? I should be done at Gram's then."

"Fine," she typed, but she wondered how she was going to stand the wait all those days in between and the early hours of that precious day. Suddenly, there was a knock at her door. Iris called out her name and Chrys said she'd be right there. "Gtg," she typed.

"Sure. C u Thurs. I'll ride over to get u."

"Ok bye."

She got up and peered into the hallway. But Iris was no longer there or anywhere else in sight. In the bathroom

Chrys took a few minutes to experiment with some makeup. She stood back and looked in the mirror. Although she barely recognized herself, she did not wash it off but headed downstairs. In the kitchen she found Iris's note tacked to the refrigerator saying she was going to Jenny's. Chrys still had her phone in hand. She held it up and stared at it, wanting the conversation with Jack to continue all the way to dinner. Oh how much they could know about each other in a few hours and how fast her day would fly! But some warning voice like a grandmother's told her not to look anxious by calling him. Besides, she added, he had taken the more chicken-ly way to contact her.

Close to dinnertime, while Chrys was unloading the dishwasher, Peri, whistling and swaggering, came sailing through the back door. He glanced at Chrys and though he didn't speak to her, she was happy he wasn't scowling. Rather, he smiled at her without baring his teeth then his smile broadened so much that he resembled a Cheshire cat with feathers sticking out the side.

"What the heck are you grinning about?" she said.

"Not much," he said opening the refrigerator and peering in. "You know, freedom is really a wonderful thing." He grabbed a small apple and bit a huge chunk out of it. Through the chews, he said, "It allows you ... such a great opportunity ... to explore and expand ... your social horizons."

"What are you talking about?" Then she caught on and her stomach went sour. "Jack! You ran into Jack?"

"Oh much more than ran into." He swung around and looked at her. "Hey, what's with the makeup? Trying out for a part as a raccoon? Or planning a career as a stripper?" He took a couple more enormous bites and grinned even more broadly.

"Oh shut up." She blinked as though something was in

her eye and picked up a tissue from the counter to wipe away some of the bottom liner. "So you ran into Jack. And?"

"Not much. We spent a couple hours together." He nibbled around the end of the apple and dropped it into the trash. "Seems like a pretty nice guy. We hit it off pretty well. Birds of a feather, I guess," he said breezing toward the door.

Chrys was on him like ego on a pop star. She raced through the house and grabbed his arm.

"What did you tell him about me?"

"Did I say we talked about you?" Peri picked her fingers off his arm as if they were leeches. "Cars. We talked about cars."

Chrysler! But Chrys had another frightening thought. "You didn't spill everything about Uncle Jules' ghost and the treasure, did you? And then have a jolly good laugh over it?"

He sniffed with snooty indignation. "Again you question my integrity," he said starting up the stairs, but at the landing he stopped and looked back. "You know, it's one thing to make me out to be some back-stabbing slime ball; it's another to say that I'd actually be a back-stabbing slime ball to Uncle Jules."

Two at a time he took the stairs, leaving Chrys in total confusion. Was this Peri's way of getting back at her? Was it all a fabrication just to prompt panic in her that would frazzle her every nerve? But what if Jack had shared information about her talk with him and so Peri had offered personal information about her in return? And if Peri had told Jack that Uncle Jules only visited *her*—what an embarrassment that would be! Why, "back-stabbing slime ball" would be too good a label! Suddenly, she felt small and afraid, as when she was six and cornered by the neighbor's dog. Like then, she could fight or she could run. This time, though, she took a deep breath and in those few seconds realized that bopping Peri on the nose probably would accomplish nothing and so would fleeing with him dogging her back. No, there was another alternative that if she remembered correctly, Shakespeare could provide.

Also taking the stairs two at a time, she scurried to her room and plucked Uncle Jules's teaching copy of Shakespeare's plays from her book shelf. She seemed to recall that the lines were in *Hamlet*. She briskly leafed through the pages. Yes! Uncle Jules had highlighted the passage and made a comment about the "beauty of the subterfuge" in the margin. Act II, Polonius says, "By indirections find direction out." How perfect. She would find out what transpired between Peri and Jack but do it without either catching on. But throughout the evening and by four a.m., she was still trying to figure out a way to work that beautiful plan.

Within the six days that followed, Jack texted her three more times, but their conversations remained on purely safe ground. After the first one, which merely confirmed their meeting on Thursday, Chrys tried desperately to push all thoughts aside of a conspiracy against her. So what if she had waited all week and Jack called on the very day Peri went to town and ran into him? And so what if Peri had looked at her with that silly grin and led her on?

The second time when Jack texted her about what chores she had to do, she wondered whether Jack wasn't offering anything personal simply because they needed to see each other face to face to do that. Chrys was thoroughly convinced that merely exchanging words on a screen wasn't really spending time together and neither of them would want to say something that could end the mutual attraction that had begun in so few minutes at Drymon's. Still, the days went by with increasing anticipation that would sometimes set her heart to dancing about the room to relieve it before it burst or else dreading that it would burst when she discovered the ugly truth of Jack's deception.

But when the third conversation again lacked anything personal, worry trampled over her like a stampede of horses. At the end of some dry talk about a movie he'd seen, she decided to use that *Hamlet* thing and let indirection discover the truth. She wrote, "So which of the new cars coming out do u like?"

"I don't know. I'm not much into cars other than wanting to have one someday. What made u ask?"

"Peri's always talking about them."

"You can say that again."

"Peri's always talking about them. lol"

"Lol Yeah, like today when I ran into him in Willow. U should have heard him run on about 4-wheel drive trucks."

"Believe me I have," she wrote. "He said u 2 spent a couple hours together. He should be all talked out for the day as far as trucks go."

"Oh, we talked about other stuff too. LOL Girls."

Chrys cringed in thinking he meant her. Hoping her fingers would take over on their own as they do on a Ouiga Board, she rested them lightly on the keys.

Finally, she wrote, "Very funny."

"Thanks."

Oh my God, she thought, he didn't get it. How could he not understand that she didn't mean that literally.

"Just teasing," he wrote, "Hey, I said I talked about 'girls' not you."

"How comforting."

"Oh great. If a guy talks about a girl, he loses. And if he doesn't, he loses too. So if there's no way to win, I guess I'm gone—"

Chrys stared at the screen for several minutes but no

more messages came. Then she kicked herself and wished she could kick Polonius, too, who had supplied zero directions about using "indirection" or how to avoid shooting herself in the foot while attempting it. Geez. She felt no better off, worse actually, now that Jack probably regarded her as some shrew with two heads and so would call off Thursday. And she still didn't know if Peri filled Jack's head with a dump truck's worth of awful or humiliating things about her. She may never know. Surely Polonius had *some* clue that the code of secrecy between guys—when it had to do with girls—was almost impossible to break.

Too quickly for Chrys, Thursday arrived. And though she had willed herself to sleep in until two o'clock so that she wouldn't have to dwell on whether her trip to Willow with Jack was still a go, she was up at nine. Iris came down an hour later looking a bit whiter than usual and strained across the eyes. Chrys, eating cereal at the table, watched her get a bowl and spoon and sit at the table.

"Are you all right?" Chrys asked. "You look funny."

"Funny, how?" Iris said picking up the cereal box and opening the lid.

"Like you're on the verge of an asthma attack."

"No, nothing like that." She put the box back down without pouring it. "I was in bed—you know—not wanting to get up yet when 'A school that's not a school,' kept repeating in my head. And then it came to me, like someone had opened up the top of my head and slipped a slide picture in." She gazed at Chrys with round eyes. "I know where to go."

Chrys put down her spoon and leaned over the table. "Yeah right. You know *exactly?*"

"Well, not the actual place yet, but I'm sure that we've got to start with a road."

"A road? The clue says 'school.'"

"But what I saw in my mind were words stretched out and skinny, like they are on a street sign. But the letters were too blurry.... " She shivered.

"What's wrong?"

"I wish I didn't get those visions. They make me feel creepy."

"I wish you didn't get them either," Chrys said not so much to comfort Iris but to express the envious wish that she get those supernatural messages instead. Sometimes Chrys passed them off as Iris's dreams or plain silliness but this vision was way too important. "Hmm, yes ... that does makes sense. The first clue could be designed to take us to a street—"

She got up, walked over to where the phone sat on the counter, and pulled out the directory from the drawer beside it. But before she opened it to the section of street names and their zip codes, she wondered how she would feel if there were many places to investigate, a "School Ave." and "School Blvd." as well as a "School St." She looked at the clock. It was almost ten-thirty and it could take a whole day by bike to scout several places. What if she should have to cancel her date with Jack? If he wasn't still peeved at her, calling off their meeting would certainly make him want to wash his hands of her for good. Still, if that intuition of Iris's was true, as it most often was, the mission had to take priority. And the others couldn't go without her. She thought nervously and prayed that if her date with Jack was miraculously still on, he would be willing to wait and do so without any explanation other than the lame, "Sorry, something came up."

CHAPTER 12

Iris walked up behind her. "Aren't you going to look for the street?"

Chrys slowly opened the front cover of the phonebook.

Iris stepped to Chrys's side and peered at her face. "Now *you* look funny," she said. "Don't you want to find Uncle Jules' treasure?"

Chrys shook off any leftover nervousness and staring at the book said, "Sure I do."

She flopped the book open to the green pages listing all the streets in Willow and their zip codes and leafed to the end. Her finger skimmed down the page, past Sanderson Ave., Scanlon St. and Schafer Ct. At the next street name her finger stopped.

"Schoonover Road," she said and looked at Iris. "No 'school' anything. Sorry."

Iris's face seemed to droop to the floor. But Chrys hesitated in sympathizing with her. Instead, she was grappling between enjoyment and disappointment over Iris's failure. True, a correct prediction would have made their quest easier. But Chrys was often compelled as she was now when the vision didn't work to tease Iris for being "pathetically normal." Their mother once took Chrys aside and convinced her that Iris's visions were the same thing as imaginary friends created to gain attention and so asked Chrys to humor her shy sister. Chrys actually took it as her mother's order to back off from having some fun with one sadly deluded soul. What their mother didn't seem to understand is that Iris regarded those visions as a frightful burden.

"Okay," Chrys said slightly perturbed for having her hopes inflated, "so it was just a dream you had this morning. So what else is new?" She nodded her head toward the table. "So finish your breakfast. Maybe you'll see something amazing in your corn flakes."

Watching Iris sit down at the kitchen table, Chrys was suddenly struck with the freedom she now had to make her meeting with Jack, provided he would show at three o'clock. But Chrys suppressed her leaping heart as she watched Iris jab at her cereal, nibble at a couple soggy spoonfuls, then dump her bowl of corn flakes into the sink and depart. Chrys vaguely felt as though she too had been dumped down a drain. But that sensation of being lifted off the ground and tap dancing up the walls and across the ceiling took over. She noted the time and seeing it was barely after eleven, actually relished having extra time. Usually, she waited until the last moment, threw on some torn jeans, stuffed her hair through a scrunchy and ran out the door. But today she felt different.

Upstairs before the mirror in her room, she carefully stroked mascara onto her light eyelashes and glided a layer of what turned out to be fuchsia gloss onto her lips. She pursed her mouth and veiled her eyes in an attempt to look sultry. Then she frowned, grabbed a tissue, and wiped her lashes and lips clean. Ugh! Positively skanky, she thought. She tossed the tube back into the drawer and rifled through the tray of others she had received as gifts for a color that would make her look, not slutty, but older—at least make her look every one of her fifteen years. Her freckly complexion had often caused people to assume that she, not William, was Iris's twin. She picked up a bottle of foundation and supposed that she could spread it on with a paver truck and cover all those freckles under a layer she prayed wouldn't crack when she smiled. Staring at the mirror, she imagined a fissure opening up across her face with the slightest grin and the San Andreas Fault cracking wide with her first laugh. She decided that even if that didn't happen, she'd only look like a fifteen-year-old who looked twelve who was trying pitifully to look twenty-five. She was screwing the cap back on, when the phone rang.

"Hi Sweetie," her mother said.

"Hey."

"Listen," she said, her voice sounding careful but urgent. "I know it's your first day off grounding, but I have a favor to ask of you."

"Like what?"

"Well, I just got off the phone with your Aunt Lydia, and she's not doing well today. I want you to go over there and be with her for a while."

Chrys glanced at her watch. "Okaaay. For how long?"

"For whatever time it takes to get her mind off Julius and..." The pause that followed made Chrys think they'd been cut off. "...and to weed her flower beds."

"Weed her flower beds? Why do I have to do that? It'll take hours, and I have to be home at three."

"For what?"

"A guy, Mom. What else?"

"Pardon me," her mother said astonished. "Then take Iris and the boys with you."

Chrys remembered that the beds were so thick with weeds the day of Uncle Jules' funeral, she could barely detect any flowers. They'd be even worse by now. She whined, "Does it really have to be today? I could go to Aunt Lydia's tomorrow early and spend the whole day over there."

"Today Chrys. You didn't hear the way Lydia talked

about Julius and cry about how he did all the outside work at their house. He always kept the yard looking so pretty. Chrys, I know it's a lot to ask, but I don't think this should wait."

"But it's only weeds."

"Chrys, it may seem that way, but they're a trigger."

Aside from her mother using the word "trigger," which gave Chrys the shivers, she didn't often feel that her mother was shoveling a guilt-trip on her. And she really didn't feel that her mother was foisting one on her now, but still, Chrys tried to picture her mother maliciously manipulating her. Try as she might, though, she couldn't.

Sighing she said, "I'll leave as soon as I can." But, she thought, not without Iris and the boys. As far as Uncle Jules was concerned, they were quadruplets joined at the head, and with that image she felt better about Iris's earlier fizzled vision. Still, the image of those flower beds came to mind too, riddling her with anxiety that even four people could get them done before suppertime, that is, provided she could get the others to move faster than snails. After all, unlike her, the boys had no plans. Their attitude would be that they can dawdle all they want. And Iris would be careful not to get too worked up and risk an attack. By God, Chrys thought, if she missed her chance with Jack over her lazy brothers and timid sister, she'd explode. She'd positively explode.

An hour later, now twelve-thirty, she had finally gotten Peri and William out of bed. Zombi-like perhaps, but at least they were moving. Within another half hour, they were dressed and heading downstairs for something to eat before leaving. And though she battled with her brothers at times so furiously that she wasn't sure she would win, Chrys was really more worried about getting Iris out of the house.

When she knocked and then peeked into Iris's room, Iris was lying on her bed, the room absent of any music and the blinds closed. Chrys hoped that she was reading, but she was flat and motionless on the bed with her face to the wall.

"Iris?" she said coming around the side of the bed, but when seconds ticked by without a response and Chrys saw Iris staring like someone paralyzed, she projected with a voice of jarring authority, "Iris, we're leaving in a few minutes to go to Aunt Lydia's."

Iris responded by pulling the bedspread over her head.

Chrys grimaced at having to wheedle Iris's involvement. She opened the blinds and got nose to nose with her sister.

"It's okay, Iris. Really. The otherworld is really very fickle."

Iris exposed her teary face. "Then I don't want to keep getting those visions."

"Tell them to go away and they will," Chrys said as she peeled away the bedspread and pulled at her to sit up. "People do that all the time with nightmares." Chrys handed Iris her shoes and said, "But you've got to say it out loud right before you go to sleep to make it stick."

Iris nodded and asked in leaving the room, "Why are we going to Aunt Lydia's?"

"It's another mission."

"Huh?"

"Mom's idea. But we're going to need gardening gloves for this one."

Surprisingly, the boys were cleaning up from breakfast when Chrys and Iris entered the kitchen. Still, Peri grumbled about why they couldn't do this later in the day; William grumbled about missing time to seek out the treasure. After looking at her watch, Chrys hustled them out the door with the assurance that Aunt Lydia needed to have family around for a while and "besides, it was Mom's orders."

They had mounted their bikes when Iris delayed them by having to go back inside for her inhaler. A few minutes later, they rolled out of the driveway and fifteen minutes more rolled into Aunt Lydia's, the boys arriving a few minutes ahead. Chrys tried not to react to their boasting when she and Iris pulled to a stop, but just the same, she resented that kind of unfair lameness. They knew she could have kept up if only Iris could. Instead of railing at them, she gave them a look that said, "Okay children, whatever," and rang the doorbell.

After a full minute Aunt Lydia had not come to the door, forcing Chrys to ring the doorbell once more and then after a couple more minutes, try it again. Chrys wondered whether her aunt was in the shower or outside in the backyard and couldn't hear it. But the yard was small and the windows were open. Chrys thought anyone outside should have been able to hear the brassy bing-bing-bong of the doorbell. She also wondered whether her mother had made sure Aunt Lydia would be home. About the time Chrys was sure they should scout the yard or step inside and call out, the door opened. In the shadows beyond it appeared a woman Chrys didn't recognize.

"Aunt Lydia?"

The door swung open but Aunt Lydia shrunk back a few steps when it did. "What are all of you doing here?" she said with the thin voice of pain.

Chrys, who had slipped on her set of gardening gloves, lifted up her hands as a surgeon does after scrubbing up. But with a wistful sound she said, "We're here to help."

Aunt Lydia nodded and waved them on, after which with her hand to her face, she sniffled several times and then disappeared. Chrys reached in and closed the front door. After delegating everyone to a flowerbed and encouraging them to work fast and be done with it, she started on her own with worry in her hands.

It was an agonizing hour of pulling weeds, not because

of the work but because of the work Chrys faced afterward to try to talk Aunt Lydia into life. Chrys knew her mother hadn't intended such measures when she called. The kids were merely supposed to show up, distract Aunt Lydia, and make her feel better by weeding the beds. But the way her aunt looked, Chrys couldn't leave without "sharing some soul" as Uncle Jules had called it—and not the invention of paper, the wheel, or white bread—claiming it was truly "the basis of civilization."

After the four of them had finished and washed up at the hose outside and more thoroughly with soap at the sink in the basement, Chyrs and the others went up. She told the boys and Iris to watch TV in the livingroom; she would talk to Aunt Lydia. None of them protested.

Chrys wandered through the house cautiously, peeking behind doors ajar or knocking gently at those closed. She eventually found Aunt Lydia sitting on the floor of the guest room upstairs and leaning against the daybed, her legs stretched out in front of her, an album open in her lap. The room was so quiet with the window shut that Chrys could hear the clock ticking on the nightstand.

"What are you doing in here?" Chrys said meekly and sat down beside her. "I've been looking for you everywhere."

Aunt Lydia looked up and around the room. "When we bought this house, this was to be the baby's nursery."

Chrys scooted closer. "I didn't know that."

"Julius and I wanted children so badly. And when we couldn't have any of our own, I tried for his sake not to want one."

"So did you think about adopting?"

Aunt Lydia dabbed at her eyes with a tissue. "I couldn't have a baby because of the complications in losing ... John. I sensed from the beginning it was a boy—turned out it was

107

too." She looked down at the album. The page featured photos of her in maternity clothes. "After that," she said closing the book, "I guess, we lost hope of having a family of our own."

"Oh. I never knew."

"We didn't want people to." She looked at Chrys. "And then your mother had you and we fell in love with the four of you instead...."

Chrys hugged her aunt for a very long time, sneakily wiping away tears that if her aunt noticed, Chrys worried might create some emotional flood that would sweep her aunt into the past forever. It was Aunt Lydia, though, who recovered her composure first and pulled away.

"And thank goodness he had his teaching. It kept his mind busy and helped him get over the loss. Until that accident out on 'School' Road, that is."

Chrys thought she hadn't heard right. "Did you say, 'School' Road?"

"Well, that was Julius's way of pronouncing it along with a lot of other people. It was really spelled S-c-h-y-u-l. Someone's last name, I think. With the 'y' sound in there, it was so awkward to say that most people slur over it and pronounce it 'school.'" She placed her hand gently on Chrys's shoulder. "Are you okay? You look kind of pale."

Chrys wanted to scream, "My God! Iris was right after all!" And an impulse swept through her to rush to the living room and tell the others, but Aunt Lydia now seemed eager to talk. Chrys gulped to drive the wave of excitement back and regain control of her voice.

"Wh ... what happened on 'School' Road?"

"A female student of Julius's at the time—he was teaching younger students then—had a fatal accident. After that happened, I thought he would fold up on himself for good."

Chrys felt a wrecking ball of anguish crash into her. "Fatal," she said as though she'd never heard the word in a newscast or heard her mother use it when talking about a patient's relapse and overdose.

"How did she die? How old was she?"

"You know, it was so many years ago and so many years since Julius stopped talking about the incident that I can barely remember it. I don't recall which of the middle school grades he was teaching that year. All I know is that her death devastated that family as well as Julius and the rest of Loyal Oak. Even with all the support this small community provided, the family moved away." She looked up with a pensive air about her and stared for a few seconds at a bare spot on the opposite wall. "It's odd that I don't remember the details. It was so vivid at the time. Now her death seems like a dream."

She sighed and set the album back on the bookshelf beside the daybed. She seemed more relaxed. Perhaps her mind was cleansed for the time of those sharply outlined dark creatures that suddenly swarm out of nowhere and flit back and forth like bats.

"You seem better," Chrys said.

Aunt Lydia patted Chrys's hand. "Much better." She sighed again and this time managed a smile. "Thanks to you and the others. You can come by anytime."

Chrys looked at her watch. It was twenty after two. If they left within ten minutes, it would be a close call to make it home in time to see Jack, worse yet if he were the kind to arrive early. Oh, this was getting too hard! Too many issues were swimming circles in her head. Too many paths she could take! Should she stay and try to jog more of Aunt Lydia's memory? But Chrys couldn't be certain whether talking further wouldn't backfire and summon those dark beasts instead of beating them back to the rafters. Should she take the time to tell Iris her vision was true to get her smiling and talking again before Chrys shared the news with the others? Should she call Jack and cancel their meeting and go directly to "School" Road to search for the treasure? And, oh no, would they have to spend more time on those stupid flowerbeds? She grappled whether she could make all of these things come out right. Frantic, but trying logically to sort out those elements, she finally realized that first things must come first.

"Come," she said tugging her aunt into a standing position. "Come see what we've done."

She led Aunt Lydia to the front door and motioned for the others to follow. Before going outside, Chrys instructed her to keep her eyes closed as Chrys and Iris took her arms and led her outside. Turning her around to face the house, Chrys told her she could open her eyes.

Aunt Lydia burst into smiling tears. "Oh, how beautiful! Just as neat and clean as Julius would have gotten them." She gave them a round of kisses in between wiping her cheeks. "You know, I just couldn't bring myself to do it."

The house did look sweet and trim, Chrys thought, and she felt proud of the others for pitching in without a lot of grumbling or slug-like slowness. The tan brick of the house with its white trim was now smiling with pink and red flowers that her uncle planted right before he got really sick. Aunt Lydia had worried at the time that the work might kill him, but he assured her that growing flowers was the best therapy. As Chrys smiled back at the house, she thought of her mother's love of flowers and her own lifted spirits in looking at them. Whimsically, she wondered whether a gene was to blame.

She breathed a sigh of relief that their work was done and done well enough for her aunt. With the anticipation of leaving, she looked again at her watch, but that was not yet in the stars. Aunt Lydia insisted on walking around the house to see the other beds to ooh and ahh over them. Rounding the front corner of the house a few minutes later, Chrys finally felt comfortable in saying goodbye.

Iris was still as quiet as she had been since they left the house. Before she got on her bike, Chrys gave her a little pinch on the arm to get her to turn her head. Chrys cupped her hand so the boys wouldn't hear and told her, "You were right about your vision!"

"Really? How?" Iris said suspiciously but with an air of excitement.

Aunt Lydia walked toward them, waving.

"I'll tell you later," Chrys said.

Iris nodded and then beamed a wide smile at Chrys.

As soon as the troop rolled out, the boys began to forge ahead. Chrys yelled at them to hold up, that she had something important to tell them. So they hung back and Chrys related the story of the girl's death and how she'd been one of Uncle Jules' students. But before Chrys could tell the meatier part of the tale, they reached the stretch of road where farms began to appear and the speed limit increased. Cars whizzed around them, making normal conversation impossible and traveling two abreast dangerous. Chrys told Iris to move deep onto the shoulder of the road behind her and then pushed to come alongside the boys, who she also ordered over and into single file. Amazingly, they complied and when she slowed her bike and motioned for them to pull over into a field where cows were grazing, the boys did that too without a complaint or jeering.

When they were all stopped and parked together, Peri said to her, "Okay, so what's so important about a dead girl that you couldn't wait until we got home?"

Instead of answering him, she turned to Iris. "That premonition of yours was right on the money. I can't believe it!"

"How? Tell me how!"

"What premonition?" Peri and William asked simultaneously.

"About a school not a school. Iris had a vision about what the first clue means and it's absolutely true!"

In recounting the remainder of Aunt Lydia's story, Chrys was surprised that Peri did not once offer anything snide, not even when she finished and they mounted their bikes again and headed out. Actually, on a quiet back road near home, all four chattered like magpies, and at times the excitement of knowing what the first clue meant raised their voices to a feverish pitch.

As they turned onto McCabe, William asked, "So why are we going home? Why aren't we heading straight for Ska-yule Rd?"

Chrys's immediate impulse was to poke fun at William for mangling the name or say laughingly, "Duh. Do *you* always carry a map of Willow?" but something old and wise deep inside her urged her not to. Instead she said, "Because I don't know where it is and I guessed that none of you do either, or somebody would've said so." Before William could ask another question, which seemed poised on the tip of his tongue, she added, "Plus, I didn't want to ask Aunt Lydia for a map and have her question me about why we needed one to go home. It would've been too complicated to talk around, and she was too upset already." Besides, Chrys said under her breath, "there's important business I have to attend to first."

The two refrigerator raiders now started pumping rapidly to outpace Chrys and Iris. Chrys yelled, "Hey, so we'll spend just enough time to grab something to eat and pack drinks if it's a long haul."

"What time is it now?" William yelled back.

112

"Twenty to."

"Then on to the treasure by three!" he shouted.

"Um ... fifteen," she called back. Then she smiled and added quietly, "Or thirty."

She turned her head and imagined that imp of guilt perched on her left shoulder, shaking its head and wagging its finger at her. She brushed her shoulder as though to knock the rascal off. Be gone, she thought. It's not like "School" Road is going to sprout legs and walk away.

CHAPTER 13

Iris had to stop within a hundred yards of their street to catch her breath and use her inhaler. So when she and Chrys reached Walden Road, Chrys suggested that she walk her bike the rest of the way. The road was not a severe slope but a persistent one. There was just enough drop from their house to McCabe Rd. to make sledding after an ice storm a breathtaking thrill. Usually, the road posed no problem for Iris, but today her asthma had been acting up. After riding to Aunt Lydia's and back and doing all that weeding while the pollen assaulted, her lungs were now rebelling.

Chrys would have ridden on, as she usually did and especially on a momentous day like this one, leaving Iris to trudge up the hill by herself, but something nagged at Chrys to get off her bike and walk alongside her sister. Yes, Chrys's heart was racing with anticipation to see Jack, and yes, she was thrilled to know the location of the first clue, but she also unexpectedly felt a special connection to Iris, a kind of protectiveness beyond the duties imposed on her as a big sister. Besides, if Jack was at the house and left before she got there, he'd have to pass them on the way.

After several yards Iris's breathing became labored, as if she'd just finished a marathon at an altitude of ten thousand feet. Another couple steps and she stopped again to catch her breath. So the two of them plodded along in silence toward home. Even though Chrys had never experienced a sense of closeness toward Iris, Chrys actually wanted to begin a bubbly conversation about Iris's poetry, her love of horses and, of course, boys. Chrys, however, kept quiet out of respect for her sister's present difficulty. Still, Chrys sprinkled their trek with moments when she laid a concerned hand on Iris's shoulder or smiled at her with reassurance.

When they reached the house, Iris looked positively spent. Chrys, not knowing how far away "School" Road was, worried whether Iris would be able to venture to it that same day. If she couldn't, Chrys vowed they wouldn't leave without her. Suddenly, Chrys hoped that Jack would be there for Iris's sake as well as her own. They'd have to schedule the trip for the following day, giving Chrys time to go to Willow with Jack and providing Iris with the time to recuperate. That scenario would be total bliss. After all, as Chrys told that imp of guilt whispering in her ear, the road would still be there, a la Shakespeare's Macbeth, "Tomorrow and tomorrow and tomorrow."

Rounding the driveway, Chrys gasped. She struggled for air as Iris did. But Iris, in her own world of distress, didn't notice. What Chrys saw ahead sticking out beyond the back of the house was the black fender of a bike. It was Jack's. Even after taking a deep breath and telling herself to be cool, she could have sworn that in parking her bike alongside his, her heart beat double. She told Iris to go upstairs and use her nebulizer if they had any hope of continuing the next leg of their journey. Chrys had dutifully plodded alongside Iris the entire length of the road and inside the front door, but when Iris took the stairs, Chrys positively glided on air through the house. In the dining room she stopped in front of the mirror above the buffet and de-smudged her eyes. Not wanting to waste time reapplying her lip gloss and risking Peri's comments in front of Jack, she merely licked them and pinched each cheek to bring on a pink tinge. Then sailing through the kitchen door, she found the three boys at the

115

table scarfing sandwiches and strawberries.

"Did you wash those first?" Chrys said staring at the carton of berries from the doorway.

"Do you have to?" William said.

"Hey, what's a little dirt?" Peri said.

Chrys marched over and grabbed the carton and a colander from a cupboard. Running the berries under the water, she said, "Dirt would actually be the healthier part. It's the chemicals, guys. The pesticides."

"Ahhh, there's chemicals in everything," Peri said.

"Yeah," William chimed in.

Chrys turned to Jack who hadn't mumbled a word thus far. "And how would you like your fruit?" She held up the strainer. "Clean?" And then she held up an unwashed quart of strawberries on the counter, "Or carcinogenic?"

He got up, smiled, and scooped a handful of berries from the colander. He picked up one last berry and handed it to her. Then he pointed toward the back door. She set the colander on the table between Peri and William and followed him outside.

They sauntered down the driveway and into the street, Jack chomping on the berries, Chrys nibbling on her lone berry. She looked at her nails and wished that she could do the same to them. But a second thought told her she would do better to file and paint them. A few minutes passed in awkward silence, then finishing the last strawberry, Jack wiped his fingers on his jeans and slipped his hand through hers.

"Sorry about the other day," he said.

A zigzag of electricity zipped through her, making her wonder if she could speak. "Me too," she choked out. "A misunderstanding."

"So are you ready to ride into town like we planned?"

Mentally, Chrys was on the road with him already,

116

joking and laughing along the way and then in Willow shopping in the art store for a frame. She was so ready to shout "Yes!" and shoot off with him that she almost forgot the other issue that day. But it came zinging back when William brayed down the road at her that it was three o'clock.

She glanced back at the house then at Jack. Moving her free hand from her face to her hips and then back again, she looked at the ground and scraped a line in it between them with the toe of her shoe. "Look, something's going on that might make it difficult for me to go."

"Like what?"

"Like you wouldn't understand."

"Try me."

Chrys was immediately thrown into a decision she hadn't expected to make. The mission was a sacred secret she felt she couldn't divulge until it was all settled. What could she say that wasn't a lie? She looked up and silently asked Polonius for some "indirection" to get her out of this mess. And then Jack did the impossible to fight against. He squeezed her hand and stopped her in the road. His soft brown eyes peered into hers.

"Try me," he said again. "I know I'm a guy, but—"

"I didn't mean that. It has nothing to do with your being a guy."

"Then what's the problem?"

William appeared again at the end of the driveway. "Come on! Iris says she's fine!"

"The problem *is*," Chrys said, "that the problem is between me and Iris and my brothers."

"So?" When she didn't immediately answer, he cocked his head and said, "Hey, are you trying to get rid of me?"

"Well, no." Chrys looked down and pawed the ground with her foot. "And yes. I ... I mean I was really looking forward to our trip into town, but there's something the four of us have to do and do together."

He slipped his hand from hers and stepped back as though to turn and leave. Chrys reached out and grasped his arm. "I just can't tell you." She tugged at his arm to make him look at her. "Can't we do this another day? Tomorrow? Same time, same place?" She grinned, hoping he'd trust her. "Jack, I promise I'll explain everything the first moment I can."

"Tell me this much, "he asked, "does this have something to do with your uncle?"

Astonished, her eyes got wide and she slowly nodded. "What makes you think so?"

"The other day when you told me about going out to his school, you had the same distant look on your face and the same spooky sound in your voice that you do now." He hooked her pinky with his own. "So okay, we're postponed until tomorrow. Same time, same place."

He had read her so perfectly she could have burst with the details, broken the secret and told him everything. Instead, she took a deep breath and directed them into a u-turn back to the house. When they got to the driveway, Chrys saw Peri, William and Iris perched on their bikes, lined up and ready to go, a small cooler slung over the handlebars of Peri's bike. Jack mounted his and sped off but not without flipping his head around and winking at Chrys, who watched him ride away feeling desperately stretched into two directions like a piece of taffy she once saw at a county fair. But Chrys, not knowing what she was doing, wondered how much this taffy pull on her heart she could bear before it came apart at the center.

"Come on, Chrys!" William yelled. "It's ten after three!"

"Who are you? The town crier?" Chrys said turning around. "What's your hurry?"

"Hey, moon-pie eyes," Peri said leaning over the handlebars, "There's always tomorrow for you two lovebirds." He smacked his lips several times with a kissing sound.

"And for 'School' Road, too!" she barked back. "You're such a creep that I have a mind to stay home."

"No," Iris piped up with a slight wheeze, "It's today. We've got to go today."

Iris didn't look at all recovered from the strenuous day. Chrys eyed her suspiciously. "Why did you say that?"

Iris leaned forward over her handlebars and peered intently at Chrys. "In my room laying on my bed with my eyes closed, I got another vision. We've got to move fast."

"Why?" Chrys asked.

"That I don't know."

So Chrys mounted her bike. William shouted, "Yee haaah!" and waved an imaginary cowboy hat above his head, and all four rolled down the driveway.

By the time they landed at the bottom of Walden, William had given directions to "School" Road. It was off McCabe, at least a six-mile journey, which would take them beyond the overpass for Interstate 71. Chrys had gone that far practicing her driving, but she couldn't recall ever biking that far. She looked over at pale Iris and now regretted using her one-time solo driving experience for going to Uncle Jules' school.

Surprisingly, after several minutes Iris was faring the trip well or pretended that she was. Part of the reason was Chrys's doing. A couple times she stopped everyone with the excuse that she herself was winded or needed a drink and so hoped to save Iris from any jeering from the boys and also preserve her physical strength. And when the road got especially steep, Chrys suggested they all save their strength and walk the hill. After almost an hour they rounded the top of the largest incline yet and whooping and hollering, sailed lickety-split down the slope. Near the bottom William pointed ahead and to the left at a street sign reading "Schyul Rd."

They skidded their tires to a stop at the bottom of the hill and stared at one another.

Then as though a string connected them, they turned their heads and peered down the straight, short, dirt road before them. On the right side was a ranch-style house with a small barn behind and a field where two cows and a horse were grazing. The land to the left appeared vacant of any dwellings but Chrys thought it was picturesque in its wildness. The only sign of mankind was a red surveyor's stick at the front corner of the property. The road was not too far away from more dense population and shopping— two miles further was Chestnut Ridge—yet Chrys guessed with all the small farms dotting the area that the size of the lot was many times larger than their three-quarters of an acre on Walden Road. Recalling Iris's love of horses, Chrys thought the open field with scattered trees looked like a great place to pasture a horse. The narrow road itself, though, was the most appealing part of the scene, fitting, Chrys thought, for a postcard or calendar. Mature oaks and maples lined the road, some of their branches interwoven like fingers. And the slanted rays of the afternoon sun shone through them, creating a soft, dappled effect on the ground like the markings on an appaloosa.

"Well?" Peri said. "Are we going to stand here all day?"

William walked forward, looking from one side of the road to the other. "A house not a house. Well, I guess we won't be tricked into thinking any kind of building will fit the riddle."

"Hey, the next clue is 'a park not a park,'" said Peri. "My clue comes next. And this sure does look like a park."

"No," Chrys said, "this can't be what Uncle Jules meant. Any piece of property like this is too close to actually being a park—any open land with trees would fit."

"Don't *all* the clues have to be here," William said, "if this is the right place? Including the last one, mine—a horn not a horn."

"He's right," Peri said smugly and tapped his finger to the side of his head. "It takes a guy to figure things out logically." He patted William on the back. "Good work, my man!"

William smiled with pride and walked on. The other three followed, each searching for anything that could be construed as one of the clues. About halfway to the end of the road, William stopped short and pointed.

"I found it! I found the house that's not a house!"

"Where? Where?" the three clamored in closing the gap between them.

Chrys followed the line of William's arm. "Oh William! That's just an ol' bird's nest."

"So? It fits the clue."

"Okay," Chrys said. "Let's lay it to rest." She turned to Peri. "Climb on up there and see."

"You're the one so anxious to find out. You do it. Oh come on, Peri," she taunted him. "You're the tough one, aren't you, who can out-bike me, out-run me, out-anything me!"

"I stoved two fingers earlier playing catch with William. I *can't* climb."

"Uh huh." Chrys said but didn't believe a word of Peri's excuse.

She was about to examine his knuckles when William whined, "I'll go then." And he lifted his leg to the notch of the trees' two main boughs and hoisted himself into it. He stood in the "V" surveying the best way to go.

The nest sat about halfway up the three-story tree and though William, not a great climber, could have wended his way to it, Chrys knew she was the better choice to reach it without breaking anything. Besides Peri would look the wimp only if *she* accomplished the task.

"Get down," she said in martyr fashion. And with the attitude of a mountain climber who has been to the top of Mt. Everest, she added, "I know exactly how to do it."

William jumped to the ground looking somewhat relieved and yet grumbling that he could've figured it out. Chrys almost said they didn't have a millennium for that, but she bit her tongue in light of the arduous journey ahead of her. Yes, she had put boys in the neighborhood to shame with her tree-climbing ability, but the distance between the limbs of this tree made it particularly challenging.

She had already lifted herself beyond the notch of the tree and onto an almost horizontal branch where she inched along until the one above it branched out and she could catch the lower one. Like an acrobat on uneven parallel bars, she swung her legs through her arms and pulled herself into a sitting position on the branch. One more limb above her and she would be close enough to see the nest clearly. But that branch was too small to carry her weight, so she scooted a few paces toward the trunk of the tree and climbed to the second limb instead, the one right above the nest.

"You're going too far," William shouted.

"Yeah," Peri yelled with delight. "You missed it!"

She waved them off and stretched herself out on the higher limb. As she crept forward, her weight bowed the branch lower and lower toward the nest. When she was directly over it, now a few feet below her, she could see it in fine detail. It was not a nest at all but a tangle of rope. In looking down from that vantage point, Chrys saw an unobstructed open space to the ground and guessed that the lump of rope was really a clumsily fashioned knot to secure a tire swing. It was now gray like the trunk of the tree and threadbare. Small twigs and dead leaves clinging to it had made the mass look like a nest when viewed from the ground.

"Well?" William shouted.

"It's not a nest." She yelled while backing down the branch. "It's a mess of rope for a swing maybe."

She looked down to see their reaction, but they weren't staring up anymore. The tops of their heads didn't tell her much, but she guessed that like her, they were all pretty well dejected.

Before she moved down to the next limb, Peri looked up and urgently waving his hands, screamed, "Wait, Chrys! Stop!"

Chrys practically jumped out of her skin. Her left foot slipped off the smooth branch. Losing her balance, she quickly shifted her entire weight onto her right foot and lunged at the trunk of the tree. Hugging its great waist, she screamed, "What is it?" With her heart pounding and her lungs heaving, she looked around and above her for a snake or a huge spider.

"From where you are," Peri yelled, "can you see all around?"

She swallowed hard. "You double creep! You scared me out of my ever-lovin' wits! What are you trying to do—get me killed? Well, with the twins as witnesses, listen up! My music collection goes to Iris!"

"Hey, I wasn't trying to get you killed. And I could care less about your out-dated music." After a second's pause he said, "Come on, will ya? Look around. What do you see from up there?"

Chrys knew it was an opportunity she shouldn't pass up, especially since she had a bird's eye view of the land on both sides of the road and since she was still harboring the feeling they were in the right place to solve the mystery. She moved branches away to scrutinize the entire expanse. Craning her neck out of joint, nothing came to view except wild grass with patches of dirt, rocks and fallen trees, or thick woods beyond the abrupt end of the road where a second red surveyor's stake was planted on the same side of the road as the one at the other end. As a last effort before she climbed down, she turned completely around and clung backwards to the trunk of the tree in order to scan the land directly behind her. In the distance she spotted a fence and so took that as the back boundary of the property. As she had surmised earlier and now with the red stakes confirming it, the size of the lot was definitely bigger than her own—four or five acres. Then scouting from the fence inward, she noted about a hundred feet from the road a deep depression in the ground.

"Well?" Peri said looking up. "What do you see?"

"Other than the usual weeds and dirt, only a hole. It looks like someone started digging a shallow lake, maybe for livestock."

"Recently?" Peri asked.

"No, it's overgrown."

She panned the land once more like a camera from side to side and top to bottom for both sides of the road then shrugged her shoulders and started down the tree. When she jumped to the ground from the crotch of the tree and dusted her hands on the seat of her jeans, everyone looked glum. As they walked back to the dirt road, no one said a thing. Each of them from time to time, though, stopped and turned around as though something would suddenly pop up to satisfy them.

The ride home seemed twice as long. Iris needed more occasions to stop and this time Chrys couldn't cover for her since her wheezing had grown loud and more frequent. Still, the boys didn't try to make Iris's life miserable for something she couldn't help and Chrys was grateful for that—almost told them that but didn't. She figured it would embarrass them into mocking Iris and so make her life miserable anyway. Chrys was also amazed that by halfway home the boys hadn't sped on, leaving the responsibility of Iris solely to Chrys. She would have thanked them for that too if she wasn't positive that saying such a thing would backfire.

Almost home now, after tromping up countless hills and peddling for miles, the gloominess of the group had seemed to work itself out. Peri asked Chrys to explain everything she had seen, to cover the ground she witnessed in excruciating detail. When she got to the description of the hole in the ground, Peri's eyes lit up.

"The accident. You said the girl died as a result of an accident."

"Yeah, so?" Chrys said.

"Maybe she drowned in that lake."

"Or maybe she got hit by a car out on McCabe. Or got struck during a thunderstorm under one of those huge trees—I saw a big lightning scar in the tree I climbed. And what would she be doing out on that property anyway? Obviously, she didn't live there. And besides, how would knowing about her death help us find 'a house that's not a house'?"

William suddenly went on a tangent about turning around and going back despite how exhausted and hungry everyone was. Finally, Iris spoke up but between gasps.

"I ... know ... it's ... there." She heaved a great breath and nodded. "You'll see."

Part of Chrys wanted to believe Iris—did in fact believe her. But the other part couldn't deny what she had seen—or rather, what she hadn't. It wouldn't hurt, she supposed, to go out to "School" Road another day. They could split up and walk every foot of the property, like people do when a child is missing, to make sure there wasn't something she had missed. Yes, she was convinced of doing that. But she wouldn't speak of it—and she prayed no one else would speak of it—until after tomorrow.

Iris's shoulders hiked high in taking her next breath. She put her hand to her chest as though somehow she could support her lungs that way. As emphatically as she could, she said, "But we must ... move ... fast.

CHAPTER 14

That evening at dinner their mother questioned why Iris appeared so weak but Iris explained, as Chrys nodded, that the weeding was what had exhausted her. Their mother, apparently satisfied with the answer, instructed Iris to go easy the following day. Their father laid down the law further by stipulating the conditions—plenty of sleep and no strenuous activity—orders that made Iris look worried. Chrys, on the other hand, was delighted to have the guilt carping in her ear silenced. She felt positively levitated off her chair with the magical prospect of her day with Jack.

A few hours after dinner, Chrys stretched out on her stomach in bed and from her nightstand picked up one of the three books assigned as summer reading. Not sure it was the kind to distract her enough from the whirlwind of the day—Iris, Jack, Uncle Jules's mystery, the dead girl—Chrys read the blurb on the back cover before diving right in. "*Looking Backward*, a vision of the future, a blueprint of the 'perfect society.'" Her kind of story. She needed something to transport her so she could sleep that night. As an added plus, it was the kind of story she loved, one that projected her through time or space or into the supernatural world. She flipped to the first page and was pretty well hooked by the bottom of it, wondering how the narrator had existed in time exactly one hundred years apart, when she heard a soft rap on her door.

"Yeah?"

"Can I come in?" Iris said.

Chrys flipped the book over, flipped herself onto her back and sat up against the headboard. "Sure."

The door opened and Iris, looking anxious, walked quickly to the side of the bed. "I can't stay here all day tomorrow. We've got to go back to 'School Rd.'"

"We will. We'll go the next day, after you've had time to recuperate. Like Mom said."

"No. It's got to be tomorrow."

"Mom will kill me if I let you ride way out there. And if you get worse—well, you might as well take my CD collection right now."

"Then I promise I'll lay down all day—I won't even ask Janice to come over—and we'll go back to 'School Rd.' late in the afternoon like we did today."

Chrys patted the bed for her sister to sit down. Chrys scooted close to her and put her arm around her. "You've got to be careful. Today was really hard on you."

Iris turned to her with an expression of surprise and then gladness. Hugging Chrys, she laid her head on her shoulder, but a few seconds later she pulled away. "I'll be fine. You'll see."

"You've gone through this before. You could need a whole day. Or two."

Usually Iris was aware of her limitations and knew to listen to the wisdom of others. Chrys, assuming she would abide this time since she rarely offered concern, rolled over and picked up her book. But Iris's hand reached over and pushed the book down.

"Not this time."

Before Chrys could object, her cell phone rang. She glanced at the screen and turned back to Iris with pleading eyes. But Iris was already at the door and as quickly as a wisp of smoke, disappeared from the room.

"Hey," the message from Jack read.

"Hey."

"Still on tomorrow?"

"Yep."

"Good, but we've got to chg. the time."

"Okay. Why?"

"Gram wants me over in the pm instead to help w/her veg. garden. She's got errands earlier."

"Sounds fine. What time?"

"How about 10? And then I'll head to Gram's at 1."

"I'll be ready." She remembered his punctuality. "10 sharp."

"U're sweet for understanding. ☺"

"☺" And she signed off.

But "sweet" kept echoing through her brain. She tried to pick up where she left off in her book but her mind kept drifting from the page. Finally, tired of going back to the beginning of paragraphs and rereading them, she put the book down. She lay back on the pillow with her arms folded behind her head and sighing, let the wonder of his words have their way with her. About the hundredth time the line swam across her consciousness, another thought surfaced. With Jack leaving by one o'clock, the return trip to "School Road" might indeed be possible if Iris was right in feeling she'd be recovered by then. Chrys sighed again. All was, indeed, right with the world. Now, if only she could sleep.

The following morning Chrys was up at nine with the help of her alarm clock. She gave no chance to fate that she'd awaken on her own in time to be her presentable best when Jack arrived. What she discovered was that an hour was way too long to consume a simple bowl of instant oatmeal and so she was left with forty-five minutes to stew over a thousand what-ifs. She moseyed into the downstairs bathroom, peered at her unadorned face, and wondered whether she should try that makeup kit one more time. But that voice telling her "not to seem too anxious" prattled on. Instead, she got her bike from the garage and positioned it outside the front door. She told that biddy of a voice that doing so was not a sign of forwardness but a signal to Jack to use the front door. Thankfully, the forty-five minutes of anguish was cut to thirty when Jack showed up early. Having kept watch through the living room window, Chrys jumped up, grabbed the bag containing Uncle Jules' gift, and ran to the foyer before he could ring the doorbell.

She swung open the door and took him by surprise. He lowered his hand from the doorbell and smiled.

"You sure *are* punctual," he said.

"We've got a really loud doorbell. You'd think Quasimoto was yanking the ropes."

"Yeah, good one," he said sliding his hands into his back pockets. "Quasimoto."

"Do you know the story, *Hunchback of Notre Dame*?" she said locking the door.

They walked to their bikes with Jack scratching his head. He flipped up his kickstand and grinned. "Is that the one about a handicapped quarterback?"

With a question like that, Chrys felt a surge of serious misgiving. My God, *he's* the doofus, she thought. But instead of uttering that and cutting their three and a half hours to three and a half minutes, she politely offered, "It's a classic by Victor Hugo about a deformed bell-ringer—"

Jack swept his arm out theatrically. "—who falls in love with the beautiful Esmeralda."

"You *do* know it!" Chrys blurted without thinking how condescending she sounded.

"Gee, I thought you'd get the joke." He pushed off and

peddled down the driveway. "I'm no doofus, you know."

"Sorry, I ... didn't mean that you were," she said and pumped hard to catch up to him. "When did you read it?"

"Freshman year. But I've got to admit that Notre Dame's a favorite team of mine so I did choose it off the list thinking it might be a sports story."

She laughed. "Easy mistake."

He glanced at her. "But knowing Mrs. Kauffman, I knew better than to think she'd include a book about football. It took me a little while to get into it, but, you know, after I finished it, I thought it was the saddest story I've ever read or could ever imagine."

Chrys looked over at him with wonder. Could he really be as honest and sensitive as he sounded? Or was he toying with her? "Indirection" came to mind and she said, "I cried for an hour when I finished it."

"I can see how a lot of people would. Talking about it actually brings me down a little. I mean, when people fall in love and no one wins—when they all die miserable—that's about as depressing as it gets."

He hadn't said he cried at the end, but what he did say was enough to convince Chrys that his heart was true. The more their minds shared, the closer she felt to him and the closer she came to confiding in him. After all, he had mentioned death and love in the same sentence. She could easily bring up the subject of Uncle Jules and his visitation. But she wasn't sure whether going from sad fiction to what could seem a scary delusion was a good idea so early in their relationship. By the time she had drawn this conclusion, Jack had moved on to talking about his grandmother and what work faced him that afternoon. He joked about stooping over for so many hours helping her plant that he'd walk away "The Hunchback of Dame Norton." Chrys, remembering some of French class, joked that since "notre dame" meant "our lady," he would actually *be* another "Hunchback of Notre Dame." They laughed so hard Chrys thought they would lose control of their bikes and run them up a telephone pole.

A minute later, still chuckling, they veered left onto the street that would take them the back way into Willow. A few more minutes and Chrys spotted the library. The arts and crafts store was only two blocks away. She suggested they park at the library and walk. Jack agreed. They could've ridden to the front of the store and chained up their bikes to a pole or a slender tree on the sidewalk, but walking would be so pleasant. After all, she was hoping that they would walk hand in hand.

And they did. As soon as they secured their bikes and she unhooked her bag, his hand found hers. Jack ran his thumb over her thumb and over the top of her hand. Chrys felt a thrill tingle throughout her. As they passed the ice cream store within the first block, Jack suggested they stop there afterwards. Chrys thought something sweet would be the perfect way to top what was becoming one of the sweetest moments in her life.

When she swung open the door to the small craft store, the bell above the door jingled. None of the few people in the store looked over. The middle-aged cashier was chattering on the phone and two elderly women were poring over the rack of embroidery thread on the right side of the store. Chrys was happy the place was almost empty and that none of the women had concerned themselves with pointing at them or giggling or even worse, saying something about "the cute couple." Without delay Chrys directed Jack to the left and into the frame aisle. He took the bag from her hand and pulled out the rolled up piece of paper. He slid off the rubber band, unfurled it, and read it quietly out loud. "'For thy sweet love rememb'red such wealth brings/That then I scorn to change my state with kings.'"

He looked at Chrys, who was browsing among the frames, trying to seem nonchalant, but in reality her heart was leaping with possibility as she listened to him recite the quote.

"It's nice. Shakespeare, isn't it?" he said still looking at it. Then he touched her arm. "You meant a lot to your uncle."

"And he meant a lot to me," she said and lifted a frame to see if the paper would fit it. "This is the one."

"What are those bugs on the corners? Dragonflies?"

"No, lightning bugs. See? The ends of their bodies are painted yellow."

He looked through the other frames on the shelf and pulled out a carved, wooden one that looked like an antique. "How about this one?"

"No. This one's perfect. The fireflies are perfect."

"How so? It has nothing to do with the quote."

"It doesn't have to. You see, we used to go to Uncle Jules and Aunt Lydia's place on Pine Lake. And at night he'd make a fire down by the water and tell us stories. One of them was about why lightning bugs don't stay lit."

"And?"

"And what?"

"Why *don't* they stay lit?"

Chrys reached back into her thoughts and tried to hear her uncle's voice. "Well, lightning bugs are too bright for their own good. They can't navigate by their own light, so they blink off to see by the light of the others and then on for the others to see by theirs."

Jack put the wooden frame back, took the one from her hands and gazed at it. "Yeah, perfect match."

They paid at the counter and left with Chrys feeling even closer to Jack. He understood her choice of a frame with fireflies without once making fun of it as so many guys, like Peri, would have. On their way back they stopped for ice cream as Jack proposed they do. She got her usual, coffee ice cream with chocolate syrup; he got chocolate chip mint with whipped cream. Tasting each other's and talking about other flavors, they moseyed back to the library.

It was during a lull in their conversation that Chrys began thinking about the mission: the "school not a school" that they had already found and the "house not a house." The answer to her clue felt so close she couldn't tell whether it was really the sweetness of the ice cream she was tasting. Apparently, she had been daydreaming so long that Jack felt compelled to ask what the matter was. She was about to say "nothing" when the light at Loyal Oak turned red and they stopped. While Jack made sure the way was clear to cross, she looked up at Drymon's Market and grew cold with excitement.

"Jack, let's stop at Drymon's for a minute, okay?"

"Okay," he said. "What do you need?"

"Not much," she said and sailed through the intersection and then left into the small parking lot.

Inside the store she told Jack he could browse; she had business with Mrs. Drymon. So he headed for the magazines on the other side of the store while Chrys stepped up to the counter.

"Hi, Mrs. Drymon."

"Hello Chrys. What can I do for you today? Some Colby cheese maybe? Or sliced ham?"

"No, I've got a question or two about this house."

"A history project over the summer?" Mrs. Drymon said picking up a bottle of cleaner and ripping off a couple paper towels.

Chrys tried to sound casual. "Something like that."

Mrs. Drymon sprayed one end of the counter.

"Did anything awful happen in this house?"

Mrs. Drymon stopped wiping and looked up at Chrys. "Who's been bending your ear with such stories?"

"No—nobody. I'm just trying to find out if something sad happened between this house and some other building."

Mrs. Drymon stopped and leaned over the counter. "Chrys, I don't know what you're looking for, but there aren't any ghosts in this house. My grandfather built this place over a hundred years ago, raised five healthy kids in it then each of my grandparents well into their eighties died in their sleep upstairs. Afterwards, rather than to sell to strangers, my mother and her brothers turned it into a store. Originally, there were the usual out-buildings—a corn crib, carriage house, outhouse and so on—but they've been gone for over thirty years now." She started spraying the other end of the counter. "Sorry, I can't be of more help to you, but the Drymon family's been abnormally short on tragedies." As she walked away, Chrys heard her mumble how people seem to assume that an old house with chipped paint and a squeaky door had to be haunted.

Jack, who had gradually moved closer through the aisles, rounded the corner of the nearest one. "What was all that about? What are you looking for?"

"We're not looking for anything."

"*We?*" He shook his head and winked. "You're slipping, Chrys, slipping big time."

She turned, walked out the door and down the steps without a word. She mounted her bike and waited with her head turned away until he was on his, then she zoomed off like a burst balloon. He followed her without trying to catch up. But when she turned onto the path through the woods that would shortcut them to Beyer Road and she got off her bike to walk, he laid on the steam and pulled up alongside her.

135

"Chrys? Where did you four go yesterday?"

She hemmed and hawed.

"Come on. Don't I have a right to know if it meant changing our date?"

"Weeelll..."

He reached over, picked up a strand of her hair near her face and ran his fingers through it. When his hand brushed her skin, a tingling raced all the way down to her toes. She stared at the ground with the hope of hiding her flushed face.

"I guess it would be okay," she said sheepishly, "just to tell you where we went. Um, way out on Mc Cabe there's a dirt road. Schyul Road, only most people pronounce it—"

"'School Rd?' That's where you went? Why? It's just a big, vacant piece of property."

She looked up at him with wide eyes. "You know it?"

"Sure. My parents were going to buy it a few years back—my mom grew up with horses and so she's always wanted to have enough land for one or two—but when she heard about what happened out there, she got more and more superstitious."

"*What* happened?"

Jack stopped, laid his bike down and sat at the base of an oak tree. Chrys did the same. He picked a wide blade of grass and ran it through his fingers over and over again while he talked.

"A girl died out there. I think it happened near the end of school because my mom said the family needed the whole summer so they'd be able to move in before school started up again. Anyhow, they had just broken ground when one of the oldest of four kids, a girl, fell and died. After that the family was so torn up—the father feeling guilty and the mother depressed all the time—that they gave up, put the property up for sale and moved away."

"Oh my God!" Chrys shrieked. "That hole! It's a basement! Oh my God, a house not a house!" She immediately felt so guilty saying so much that she quickly tried to subdue her voice to that of a reporter. "Jack, do you know how the girl fell?"

"Don't know that part of the story. Say, can you tell me now what this is all about? What's a house not a house got to do with anything? That doesn't make any sense." Suddenly, his eyes lit up. "Drymon's. That's why you stopped to talk to Mrs. Drymon. That's also 'a house not a house.'" He placed his hand on the top of hers. "Come on. You can trust me."

The imp was back on her shoulder demanding that Chrys keep her mouth shut, but the moment felt so right. And he knew so much already. There was no telling how much more he could offer. Mentally, she flicked the imp away as though it were a pesky fly.

"All right. I'll tell you as much as I can, but you've got to promise not to let on to my brothers and sister that you know anything. And you can't think I'm crazy, either."

He crossed his heart and nodded solemnly. After dropping the blade of grass, he picked up her hand and squared himself to her to give her his undivided attention. Starting slowly, she shared with him about the night Uncle Jules visited each of the children, the mission he had given them to accomplish, the first two clues and how "School Road" and the foundation of the house partially satisfied the first one. At the end of the story, he looked questioningly at her.

"But you said the second clue had to do with two houses, both places of great sorrow. The dug basement is only one of those. What do you think the other might be?"

"I don't know but we're planning on going out there again today to find out," she said getting up and dusting herself off. An afterthought raced between her lips and she looked back at him. "What was the girl's name?"

"Don't know that either, but I know she was twelve when she died. That's why my mom got so spooked about buying that land. During the time they were considering it my younger sister turned twelve." After a moment's pause, he said, "What were the other two clues?"

"Oh, I don't think I should tell you that until we find them."

"I understand." After a pause he said, "And I don't think you're crazy."

She smiled broadly at him. Though they strolled the rest of the way through the woods in silence, Chrys could feel an invisible thread of affection drawing them closer together. She looked down and wishing her polo wasn't so loose, she pulled it to her back and smoothed the wrinkles in front.

At Beyer Road., before getting on her bike, she said, "Thanks for being so sweet."

He smiled broadly. "My pleasure."

They mounted their bikes and took the washboard road at an old dog's pace so they could still talk. He sighed as a sign, it seemed, that he was about to change the subject.

"Chrys? How did you get your name? I mean the way it's spelled."

She cringed. Why did he have to ruin a perfectly wonderful afternoon by bringing up the bane of her existence? And what could she do? If she refused to answer, he would only grow more curious, and yet the truth was so hokey, she'd never live it down if she told him. It would be worse, she thought, than dealing with "Chrysler."

"You were right all along," she said. "It had something to do with the backseat of a car."

Jack laughed boisterously. "At least *I* know a joke when I hear one. Now, what's the real reason?"

She was caught between a marble slab and a granite

boulder. She cringed again and said in a low voice, "I was named after a flower."

A second ticked by as he digested her answer. Then his eyes got big. "Oh, I get it!" he yelled as though he'd discovered gold. "You're Chrysanthemum!" He bopped his forehead lightly with the heel of his hand. "Of course! There's Iris too!"

"Yeah," she said, wishing all her petals would shrivel up and die.

"But what about the guys?"

"They're flowers, too. 'Peri' is from periwinkle and 'William' comes from sweet William."

"Hey, that is too cool! But why flowers?"

"My mother loves growing them. She picked her favorites based on their strong qualities."

"So that's why Peri calls you Big Flower! That is just too cool."

"Yeah, you think so? Well, I wouldn't remind my brothers of any of this if I were you unless you want to become 'Big Bruise.'"

They were home by now, thank goodness. And thank goodness it was almost one o'clock. After a quick snack he would go on to his grandmother's and plant tomatoes. Her name was "too cool," huh? Mortifying, might be a better explanation. Oh, why did she confide such a thing? How could she bear to hear him say her name again? And heaven forbid that he tease her about it or ever call her "Big Flower," especially in public! She had to make her mother see the light and agree to let her change her name. Somehow, Chrys must make her understand that—according to Uncle Jules—there was more than one way to die.

CHAPTER 15

After waving Jack goodbye and going upstairs to weep over the indignity of her name, Chrys found a note from her mother taped to her bedroom door. Her mother must have forgotten something and doubled back after Chrys had left. Too bad she couldn't have forgotten her expectation for Chrys to get a summer job.

The note read,

> Sha na na na, sha na na na na,
> Sha na na na, sha na na na na,
> Yip yip yip yip yip yip yip yip
> Mum mum mum mum mum mum
> Get a job.

Funny, very funny, Chrys thought. She had a comedienne for a mother. *Not*. But the hilarity of the note went way beyond those awful lyrics from the Silhouettes. Following was an explanation pointing out how three weeks of summer had passed and so Chrys needed to spend the day looking for employment if she wanted "to drive the car beyond what fumes remained in the gas tank, buy clothes at the end of the summer, go to the college of her choice or retire before she lost all her teeth." Chrys got the vague impression that her mother was coming out of her deep depression. Actually, she relished her mother's tongue-in-cheek comments. They were a sign of her re-entry into life, as though after weeks of being submerged, her head had finally appeared above a stormy sea and she drew her first saving breath. Since Uncle Jules' death she had seemed so solemn, so near tears that Chrys wondered if her mother was going to be stuck in neutral forever. But after that conversation about changing her name, her mother often gave her sidelong glances, as though she was sizing up a mental patient. So, though her mother seemed in better spirits, Chrys decided to put the issue of her name on a back burner.

She glanced again at the handwritten note and now winced at the prospect of fulfilling it. But at least her mother hadn't done any footwork for her, listing places to apply or calling ahead and arranging interviews, like at the craft store, for instance. Her mother may have known the owner and been able to pull strings to get her employed there, but the last way Chrys wanted to while away the summer was to talk to old women about yarn or try to figure out for some eight-year-old boy how many wooden Popsicle sticks it would take to build a three-foot replica of the Eiffel Tower. Chrys pulled the note off the door, grabbed a pen from her desk, and in the space at the bottom jotted down some respectable possibilities: Ice Cream Supreme, Old Navy, Stan's Sandwich Stop, and Willow Public Library. She held up the list and nodded at her choices. She would start, of course, with the most tantalizing of the four.

With the boys still asleep at one o'clock and Iris lazing in front of the TV on the living room couch for the rest of the day, Chrys actually felt bored enough to follow her mother's order to search for a job. She folded the list and stuffed it into her pants pocket. All the stops would be in Willow. Even though Drymon's Market would have been enormously convenient, she had dismissed that as a possibility after yesterday's embarrassing moment.

On her way out, Chrys explained to Iris where she was headed. Iris gazed at her woefully, but Chrys assured her that she'd be back in a flash—in plenty of time to ride out to "School" Road—though Chrys knew the trip out there was about as probable as seeing frogs fly. She smiled at Iris, patted her shoulder and asked if there was anything she wanted before she left. When Iris shook her head, Chrys pointed toward the kitchen and reminded Iris of the lunchmeat and leftovers in the fridge, that Iris had to rest, take her meds and eat if she were to regain her strength. Iris crossed her heart.

Chrys's first stop, the place where she most wanted to work, was also the first she came upon as she rode into Willow—the library. She gazed at the red-brown brick of the building and the great pointed arch of an entrance with six more recessed arches within it that led to the double front doors. She chained up her bike outside and walked through the great wooden doors as though walking into another world. The smell was the first thing to transport her. The scent of dog-earred old books and that of crisp new ones mingled together into a perfume of human history and possibility. Stepping in farther, she was moved by another force. The great quiet spoke of the sounds and sights going through individuals' heads who were sprawled in over-stuffed chairs with a paperback in their laps or stooped over volumes laid out on the hard wooden tables. Other than her room, there was no other place where she felt more at home. The best part of the job, she imagined, would be snatching up books before the public could check them out. She hated waiting for a book. It was an awful feeling to be told that the only book that could quench her present thirst wouldn't be available for weeks. Her mother had often suggested she buy the book with her allowance, but Chrys's library only consisted of books purchased after she had read them and loved them. She wanted none of her money spent on what didn't move her.

She approached the woman at the counter and asked for an application. The woman shook her head and said they weren't hiring. However, would she like to volunteer? Chrys would have said yes if she could, but instead she thanked the lady and left.

Her next stop in descending order of desire was the deli. She was a hoagie connoisseur, so the idea of making sandwiches for others appealed to her. But that store was finished hiring for the summer. On to the ice cream store, but with the same luck. Walking the next block to Old Navy, her last ditch attempt, she was beginning to worry. After crossing the street, though, she noticed a sign in the window: "Part-time help wanted."

"Oh well," Chrys said opening the door, "it may not be my first choice, but fifteen per cent off a raft of new school clothes is nothing to sneeze at." She looked down at her usual clothing fare—plain jeans, sneakers, and another loose polo. "Hmmm," she said staring at a female manikin in the window which sported embroidered khakis, 3" silver platform flip-flops, a white cami with a black shrug over it, and perched above it all was a silver necklace with a small locket. She struggled to imagine herself in that outfit, to see herself with her curves showing. But the shoes broke her spell—those God-awful shoes—

She went in and filled out the application then spoke with the manager, who asked her if she could start Monday and whether she'd be willing to work some hours after school started. She seemed pleased with Chrys's positive responses and said she'd get back with her over the weekend. Chrys, feeling the job was a done deal, cordially thanked the manager and said she'd wait for her call.

By the time Chrys got home it was almost three. The boys were up and surprisingly, dressed. Iris, gone from the downstairs couch, Chrys found minutes later in her bedroom writing in her diary and looking remarkably healthy. Her face had color, her eyes shone, and her body shifted with a kind of pent up energy.

Masking her astonishment, Chrys said, "You seem better."

Iris bounced in turning in her seat. "I'm *all* better. So when do we leave?"

Chrys sputtered, "I ... I ... I"

"We are going aren't we? We have to go."

"Oh, Iris. I don't know if we should take that kind of chance—especially with what Mom and Dad said."

Iris stared at her. "Look at me. Do I look sick?"

Chrys was so taken aback by her sister's boldness that she couldn't speak. She wondered whether Iris hadn't been magically transformed to carry out the mission she'd seen as urgent. Such mystical rejuvenations happened in many of the books Chrys had read. Maybe Iris was being driven by supernatural forces to fulfill her vision. Chrys debated her parents' directive to keep Iris at home. If Iris's vision was true and time was running out, then Chrys had to allow the trip to "School" Road. And if the trip didn't pan out, nothing would be lost, especially since Iris seemed a hundred and ten per cent.

So Chrys rounded up the boys and cautioned them and Iris to follow her orders, not only to keep Iris safe but also keep all of them out of trouble. If they came back with Iris any worse than when their mother last saw her, all of them would be grounded for the rest of the summer and the mission would be sunk. The three of them solemnly swore allegiance, satisfying Chrys's raw nerves. The boys packed a cooler with drinks and Iris went upstairs for her inhaler. When they trailed out the back door, Chrys was the last to leave. Hesitantly, she lifted the kickstand of her bike and pushed off.

After stopping three times over the first half of their journey, Chrys was amazed at how well Iris was doing, though she did seem unusually jumpy. But Chrys, both anxious and excited, assumed Iris was experiencing those emotions as well. What also amazed Chrys was that again the boys stayed close to them and didn't complain about stopping so frequently. And not once did either of them urge Iris to peddle faster.

The second half of the trip was equally as successful. Chrys used the time to clue in her siblings about the information Jack had shared. When they came down that final hill everyone was brimming with enthusiasm. But when Chrys looked over at the expanse, she was shocked at the change.

"Hey, cool!" William shouted. "The grass is cut!"

"Yeah," Chrys said, "It does look like a park now."

"See!" William shouted. "A park not a park! I told you! This *is* one of the clues."

"I don't think so," she said. "'Not a park' means 'not at all like a park. I mean, this road is no school and a hole in the ground is no house. And you can bet that 'a horn not a horn' is not going to be something that produces sound. They're all games with words."

"Well," William said disappointedly, "it's still better than walking in knee-deep weeds."

"I wouldn't jump up and down about that either just yet," Chrys said.

"Why not?" Peri said.

"Because the grass is still tall enough to miss something small."

'Uncle Jules wouldn't have given us clues that weren't possible to find," William asked, "would he?"

Chrys wasn't sure about that. She was beginning to doubt that Uncle Jules had visited them at all. As she had read in a book once, seeing their uncle could have been a case of mass hallucination. Perhaps her mother's suspicions were right.

They had walked halfway down the road, almost to the huge tree that Chrys climbed the day before when Iris suddenly ran ahead a little way, past the tree. Pointing at something near the ground, she yelled, "Oh, look at this!"

The three of them ran over. Planted in the ground on the other side of the tree was a builder's sign. Chrys recalled the red surveyor's stakes at the corners of the property and kicked herself for not taking note how new they were. Had she made the connection, she would have suggested they stay longer yesterday and walk the acreage then. Not knowing when the ground-breaking would begin, Chrys urged the other three to search slowly and carefully. According to Iris's vision, they had no time to lose to find the other "house that isn't a house."

She suggested they spread out in a straight line from the front of the property to the back and walk the length of it, sidling over a couple feet after each pass to make sure no clod of dirt was overlooked. It was a tedious process but a cool one since the sky was overcast. Within an hour they had covered every square foot of the acreage, including the bottom of the deep hole. Standing in it gave Chrys an eerie and sad feeling that she couldn't explain and didn't want to for Iris's sake. Climbing out, Chrys realized the mature trees behind it would have set off a house well. Marching between the trees and the hole, she instructed the others to scout the same distance beyond the "basement" on the three other sides one more time before they packed it up.

Fifteen minutes later they were finished and back on the dirt road. From their silence and bowed heads, Chrys suspected that she was not the only one with a heavy heart. Iris stopped again in front of the builder's sign.

"I don't understand," she said. "I thought sure we'd find something if we came out here right away." She looked at Chrys with worry. "Maybe we're already too late."

As they mounted their bikes, their faces transformed into ones of downright hopelessness. The cloak of silence the twins and Peri seemed to be wearing as they rode along McCabe made Chrys so want to scream out of frustration that she actually did. The others stopped in the road and looked at her.

"It's okay," William said. "It'll be all right. Something always turns up."

Iris, looking worn, nodded.

"Yeah," Peri said sincerely. "We can't lose our heads. Now's the time to put them together."

Chrys couldn't remember the last time he said something so kind. She would have hugged him if she felt he would have let her.

"But what if the land's all torn up tomorrow?" Chrys said. "It'll be over."

"There's no use thinking about something we're not sure is gonna happen," Peri said. "When we get back, we'll all sit down and go over everything we *do* know. Okay?"

Iris and William nodded exaggeratedly at Chrys. She ran her hand through her hair and looked back over the way they had come.

"Maybe we should have criss-crossed over the property, too. Maybe we missed something."

"Not an inch escaped us," Peri said. "You did just fine, Big Flower. We all did just fine."

Usually, she would have been offended at his calling her that, but he said it so differently this time that she dismissed it. She glanced back at the group and sighed in resignation. Then she nodded, suggested they move on and that they meet in her room right after dinner. The others smiled and peddled off.

Within a mile from home, Iris was not looking well. She leaned over the handlebars in an attempt to open her airways and her face looked strained and pale. Chrys questioned whether she was experiencing any pain, but Iris shook her head. Chrys suspected she was being stoic. And for an asthmatic, denial could be deadly. Chrys looked at her watch and suggested Iris take a puff from the inhaler. Iris shook her head.

"Why?" Chrys asked. "It's time."

"I can't," Iris said strangely.

Chrys eyed her narrowly. "Why *can't* you?"

Iris cringed and in a tiny voice said, "I doubled the dose."

Chrys screeched her bike to a halt. "Stop right there! You did what?"

"Before we left the house I used my inhaler twice."

"My God! Why would you do such a thing?"

"Well, I figured if one puff helps then two would help even better."

"That's why you were so hyper! That was really stupid, Iris. I'm surprised you'd do such a thing. You know how important it is to follow your meds. Exactly."

"I know," Iris said sheepishly and lowered her head. "But we had to move fast."

"Well, we're not going to be moving at all once Mom catches on to this."

"I'll be fine," Iris said wheezing more noticeably.

"Yeah, you keep saying that."

Iris knew to rest when they got home and use the nebulizer in her room. Meanwhile, Chrys bit her nails to the quick in anticipation of what her mother would say and do if she became suspicious about why Iris had not improved. The hour dragged on. Neither reading nor music could sail her mind away. Finally, at five-thirty her mother pulled her car into the garage and a few minutes later "Yoo-hooed" in entering the back door. Chrys greeted her at the kitchen door. They exchanged hellos and Chrys helped her mother with her briefcase and the bucket of chicken for dinner. Then when her mother sat down at the kitchen table, took off shoes, and stretched out in the chair, Chrys sat down also and leaned across the table. Her mother arched her shoulders to get out the kinks.

"Bad day?" Chyrs said.

Her mother leaned her head back and closed her eyes. "Sometimes it seems as though there are no good ones anymore." When she opened her eyes again, they were moist with tears.

She took a great breath and said, "I miss him. Every minute of every day." She looked at Chrys. "Don't you miss him?"

"Of course I do. It's just that..."

"Don't say it. I don't want to hear again that he's still with us." She gave Chrys one of those long, concerned stares. "I think I'm going to make an appointment for you with Dr. Belmont."

"Dr. Belmont? But he's the adolescent psychiatrist you work with!"

"And I think you could use his help in the grieving process."

"No I don't. I'm just fine. And don't treat me and look at me like I need a strait-jacket."

"Chrys, you know I didn't mean it like that.... I just worry that you've yet to shed a tear over your uncle's death."

Suddenly, Iris appeared at the door, but seeing their mother, she turned to walk away.

"Come here, Honey," their mother said with concern written across her face.

Iris turned around and came over, glancing stealthily at Chrys. Their mother tipped up Iris's chin to look at her straight on and leaned forward to hear her breathing.

"You don't seem much better," she said looking more worried. "You don't look better at all."

Another furtive glance passed between Chrys and Iris.

Their mother looked up at Chrys. "What do you know about this? How did she get worse?"

"We ... we just took a little bike ride, that's all," Chrys said.

Her mother stood up. "Where to?"

Iris backed up toward the kitchen door. "You stay here," her mother said to her sternly. Then to Chrys, "Well?"

"We heard about some accident out on McCabe and went to check it out."

"How far out?"

"Oh, just beyond the overpass."

"You call that a little bike ride?" her mother yelled. "You let your sister who's not well ride that far?"

"She seemed fine by this afternoon, really."

"Really, I *was*," Iris chimed in.

Her mother sat down in the chair again only this time she slumped into it as dead weight. Her shoulders shook and tears spilled over. "I feel like we're coming apart. I mean, the four of you have never been close, and I've never understood why, but it's like the whole family is disintegrating—the constant snipes at one another, then taking the car by yourself and now this with Iris—how could you be so thoughtless? How could all of you be so thoughtless?" She put her hand to her mouth and sobbed a few times. "Things were so much better when Julius was alive. Since he died, we've been coming apart just like the Peck family after they lost poor little Allison." She sobbed again.

Chrys's heart began pounding. She walked behind her mother and put her arms around her neck. "No, we're fine. We're not coming apart. Really, we're not. And I'm sorry about Iris. We thought she was perfectly okay." Her mother seemed calmer, but Chrys could feel her mother's continued agitation in the tight muscles of her back. Though a surge of adrenalin was prickling through Chrys's body, she began to massage her mother's neck. Trying to keep from shaking, she said, "Mom, who were those people you were talking about? And who's poor little Allison?"

Her mother succumbed to the soothing influence of Chrys's hands and hung her head. "They were a family who rented the two-story at the end of our street while they were building a house. We only knew them for about a month."

"Building where and how long ago?"

"Way out on McCabe. It was the year you were born."

Chrys's heart leaped. "Right on McCabe?"

Her mother glanced back at her. "Why do you ask?"

"You've never mentioned them before, that's all. I thought I knew everybody who ever lived around here."

Chrys worked harder on a knot in her mother's right shoulder, making her mother groan with satisfaction.

"So where was it on McCabe?" Chrys asked as nonchalantly as possible.

"Well, part of the property bordered McCabe but most of it was off a little dirt road."

Chrys stopped rubbing for a second. "What road?" And she held her breath.

"Let's see, was it Palmer? No, the one before it—School Road."

Chrys's mind reeled and her heart beat so furiously she could barely emit a sound. Finally, she said, "How did the girl die?"

"She fell from a tree." She ran her hand over her face

and then the tips of her fingers rested on her lips. "Or was it from a tree swing? I don't remember which." Her eyes welled up with tears again and her throat caught in saying, "Her death at the age of twelve absolutely destroyed that family, just like my brother's death seems to be tearing ours to shreds too." She paused in thought. "Allison was the youngest in the family."

Iris's face registered sheer fright and she whispered, "And she was twelve."

Chrys's mind was flashing pictures of the huge tree from the day before, perspectives from the ground looking up and one showing the unobstructed drop from high in the branches. Then her mind played her a scene of a girl on a swing attached at that great height and the girl sweeping to ten feet in the air at the uppermost point.

A heaving sound from Iris suddenly stopped the onslaught of images and Chrys looked up at her sister. After several more gasps for air, Iris's skin began to drain of color. While her face quickly paled to the shade of flour, her lips and fingertips turned as blue as fresh bruises. Chrys's mind searched for an answer to Iris's sudden deterioration. Then it came to her—Iris had creeped herself out with this new information. Yes, the girl's age. That was the culprit. Chrys realized Iris had not known the girl's age was the same as her own.

Now struggling to take a breath and hunched over in obvious pain, Iris suddenly rushed to the freezer, flung open the door and plunged her head inside. Their mother's head jerked up and her gaze locked on Iris.

Grabbing Chrys's hand and rising, she said, "Pull my car out and bring it to the front of the house. I'll run up and tell the boys we're on our way to the hospital."

CHAPTER 16

The only medical facility in Willow, other than the halfway house, was a walk-in clinic. So they would have to transport Iris to Chestnut Ridge Memorial Hospital seven or eight miles west on McCabe. And in doing so, they would go right by "School" Road.

Iris was in the passenger seat with the air conditioning blowing at her full bore while Chrys was in the backseat leaning forward to try to calm her. She told Iris to picture herself floating on a raft on a sunny summer day on Uncle Jules' lake and kept assuring her that she'd be fine, an ironic comment for Chrys to make after taking Iris's use of it so lightly.

They were over halfway to the hospital when their mother looked at Iris and inspected her. "Is it any better after using the inhaler?"

Iris shook her head.

"You had her use the inhaler before you left?" Chrys asked.

"I thought it might help." She reached over and turned Iris's face to her. "But I think she's too constricted."

A wave of concern rolled over Chrys about the double dose earlier. "Would it matter when she used it earlier today?"

"Iris told me it was several hours ago, so it wouldn't make a difference even if she could breathe in the medication." In the pause of Chrys's wild relief, she went on.

"I had a hunch that if she was bad enough to need the freezer, the inhaler probably wouldn't work. But it was worth a try." She made a circle with her thumb and forefinger. "Picture a nickel as the diameter of a normal trachea. Now picture a cocktail straw. That's Iris's airway right now."

She asked Chrys if she recalled the one other attack that was serious enough to rush Iris to the hospital. But Chrys was six at the time and remembered only a flurry of loud voices, a great deal of rushing about, and her father's driving the two boys and herself to Aunt Lydia and Uncle Jules' house to spend the night while her mother drove away with Iris.

Chrys peered at Iris who was bent at the waist, her mouth gaping, lungs heaving for oxygen and her hand clutching her chest. Chrys for the first time knew she had no way of truly understanding the panic and the pain her sister was experiencing, but it was also the first time she had really tried to. Remembering Iris's remarks a few times about feeling pain all the way through her chest, Chrys put her hand on Iris's back and rubbed it gently. Anything to get Iris's focus off "School" Road and that twelve year old girl. Chrys knew that the worse Iris became, the more she would be able to picture herself with the same fate—and the closer she'd come to it. Chrys suggested that her mother turn on the radio to Iris's favorite station. A song in progress came on, one that Chrys knew, so she sang it softly while she stroked Iris's back, hoping to plant something pleasant in Iris's mind.

Chrys had never known her mother to speed but she seemed to take those back roads like a Formula One racecar driver through the mountains of France. Maybe she thought a police escort wouldn't be such a bad thing. At any rate, they arrived about fifteen minutes later at the hospital emergency entrance. Her mother pulled into a parking spot near the main doors. Getting out, she instructed Chrys to come to Iris's other side. Together they put her in a wheelchair and pushed her through the doors.

Three other people were waiting for assistance. One woman held an ice pack to her bloody mouth. A young girl of about eight, cradled in her mother's arms, looked green as though nauseous. The third, a man in his thirties, sat with one shoe off, his right ankle triple the size of the left one. On the other side of the room, a woman behind an oval reception desk took one look at Iris, stood up and came over. Their mother explained that she was asthmatic and having an attack. The woman looked at Iris's lips and hands, said she'd be right back, and scurried down a hall. A few seconds later a man and a woman appeared, both registered nurses, as their name tags indicated, and dressed in blue hospital uniforms. The male nurse was pushing a gurney. While the man raised the back of the stretcher so Iris would be sitting up, the female nurse asked questions of their mother—what maintenance medications she was on, the time of the last aerosol usage, previous hospitalizations, the last time she was administered steroids, when the exacerbation began, and what precipitated it. That last question is what perked up Chrys's ears along with their mother's answer that Iris had over-exerted herself.

As they whisked Iris away down that same hallway, Chrys asked her mother, "Why did they want to know what started the attack?"

"Because treatment is different if an allergy or some illness, like a cold, sets this off rather than exhaustion or anxiety."

Chrys suppressed her sigh of relief. She didn't have to say anything about Iris's freaking out, after all. Opening up the whole issue of Uncle Jules' mission might ruin everything. And freaking their mother into a nervous breakdown wouldn't help any either. The receptionist asked their mother for an insurance card, gave her a clipboard with papers, and told her she could go back to room "5," where Iris was being taken, to fill them out. Chrys asked if she could go, too. The woman patted her arm and nodded.

A woman doctor in a white coat and two other people were hovering over Iris when Chrys and her mother rounded the corner of the room. The doctor was listening to Iris's chest. One of the others, a young man, was hooking up tubing to an oxygen machine. The doctor stepped back and the man inserted the ends of the tube in Iris's nostrils and turned on the machine. The third person, the same nurse who assessed Iris in the waiting area, was tapping the top of her hand. Chrys quietly asked her mother why she was doing that. Without looking up and before her mother could answer, the nurse said she was trying to get a vein to plump up so she could start an IV. After that, Chrys silently watched and listened in awe at the bustle in the room. Less than a minute later, still another person, a heavy-set man with a walrus mustache, entered the cramped space "to draw blood for blood gases" he said. He told Iris the test would tell how much oxygen was in her bloodstream, and then he warned her that it might hurt some since he'd have to use an artery. Their mother rose and held Iris's hand as he wiped her thin wrist with alcohol. When he stuck her, she stiffened and screeched. Tears rolled freely down her face.

Through all this their mother didn't flinch. She also didn't make a sound. The clipboard of papers lay on the floor under her chair. Maybe she was too afraid, Chrys thought, or maybe she felt comfortable with what they were doing. Maybe she didn't want to ask questions that would distract them. Chrys guessed that probably all those reasons held true. Although when her mother sat down again and Chrys reached for her hand, she gripped Chyrs's tightly. Her mother's hand was so cold Chrys shivered at the thought of anyone holding a corpse's.

After ten minutes of the doctor's examination and her ordering tests, she turned to their mother and extended a hand, which her mother shook.

"I'm Dr. Morris. And first things first—Iris is going to be just fine. We've got her stabilized with oxygen and a steroid in the IV. But I'm afraid she won't be ready to go home today. We still need to do a chest x-ray to make sure she has no congestion which could complicate her condition and set up respiratory therapy every four hours."

Chrys asked, "How long will she be here?"

"Well, her attack is considered moderate, so if she responds really well to the medication and treatments, two or three days. If not, it could be closer to a week."

Chrys silently prayed for two days.

"Any other questions?" the doctor asked, moving her gaze from their mother to Chrys.

"No," their mother said. "Thank you."

Dr. Morris walked to the door and turned around before leaving. "They'll be moving Iris to a room in a minute or so. By the time you finish with the admitting desk, she should be settled in."

Her mother finally breathed deeply. She went over to Iris, patted her arm, and repeated to her that she was going to be fine and that they'd see her again in a few minutes. She told Chrys to pick up the clipboard and they left. Walking back to the waiting area, her mother put her arm around Chrys and rested her head against Chrys's. Filling out the papers, though, she still looked worried and Chrys noticed that her handwriting wasn't as smooth as it usually was. When she was finished, she handed the clipboard of papers to the lady at the reception desk, who with a gentle voice gave her Iris's room number.

When they got to the room, Iris was propped up in bed in the traditional hospital gown. The tubing for her IV and oxygen draped across her and over the side of the bed, making sleeping on her stomach, her favorite position, absolutely impossible. Chrys worried that if she couldn't sleep, she wouldn't recover in time. But when Chrys focused on her face, which no longer looked as pale as a biscuit, she felt more positive about Iris's ability to be released after just two days. Iris's pink lips parted and she smiled as the two of them entered.

"How are you doing?" their mother asked, though it was obvious to Chrys that instead of this question an enormous sigh of relief was more in order.

"I'm fine now," Iris said.

Their mother came over and gave her as big a hug as all the tubing would allow and ran her hand along her face. "Please don't ever do anything again that would put you into this kind of danger and scare us to death this way."

Chrys caught the irony of that, too, for Iris had almost scared herself to death.

Iris looked into her lap and fidgeted with her fingers. "I won't."

"Well," their mother said patting her arm, "I'm going to call home and let the guys know you're out of the woods." She turned around and zeroed in on the nurse's station outside.

Iris turned to Chrys. "Thanks."

"For what?"

"For not telling about my double dose. I don't want us all to get grounded."

"That's okay." Then she said sternly, "Besides taking your meds the way you should, you've got to try really hard not to get upset with the rest of the stuff we may find. I mean, we've got two—two and a half—more clues to

158

uncover. Plus the treasure itself." Chrys leaned over her and lowered her voice. "Coming here, we passed right by that property and nothing's changed. I don't think we're too late. But we will be if you're going to freak yourself into an asthma attack about everything that comes up."

Iris crossed her heart. "I'll be fine. I promise."

Chrys quickly rolled her eyes at Iris's standard wording but then high-fived her. "Okay then," she said and smiled.

"Your father and the boys just arrived," their mother said re-entering the room.

"Well, I guess I'll go sit in the lobby downstairs," said Chrys. "There'll be more room." She gave Iris a hug, squeezed her hand, and winked at her. "You work on getting better and coming home."

Iris winked back and nodded.

Outside the room their mother caught Chrys's arm. "Why did all of you go where you did today? And why the questions about the death on School Road?"

Chrys shuffled her feet.

"It has to do with Julius, doesn't it? You would risk Iris's life over wishful thinking, a dream—or a delusion?" She handed Chrys a card. "You're seeing Dr. Belmont on Monday."

"Not Monday, pleassse."

Her mother clasped Chrys's shoulders. Softly she said, "It's for your own good."

As her mother walked away, Chrys glanced at the card. "Twelve o'clock. Great. Just great."

Chrys passed their father and the two boys in the hallway to the elevator. Chrys told their dad to go on; she wanted to talk to Peri and William for a second. She motioned them to an isolated corner of the hall away from the elevator doors. She relayed the scene at the house with their mother—how upset she was about their taking Iris with

159

them on their bike ride, the story of Allison the dead girl and how she fell from a tree or a swing, what year it took place, and how all that had served to freak Iris into an asthma attack. She included every detail to make sure the boys wouldn't say or do anything that would trigger another such episode for their mother or catapult Iris into intensive care. She especially warned them to be sensitive about Iris in regard to the mission—even after she was home.

"It's Monday we've got to worry about," she said. She didn't dare mention her appointment with the shrink. "No one's going to grade that property over the weekend, but come Monday they could. And we want Iris well by then."

"We'll just do it without her then, over the weekend," was Peri's simple solution.

"We can't. All of us have to be there. Didn't we all agree?"

"But she's bogged us down already." Peri reached over and patted William on the back a couple times. "And if this weekend is going to mean the difference between finding the treasure or having it bulldozed to pieces, then I say let's move on without her."

"Yeah," William said, nodding. "I vote for a whole treasure."

Peri turned William around toward Iris's room. "Come on."

Feeling like a frustrated child, Chrys stomped her foot. "Ooooh," she grumbled, "you're both creeps. How are you going to sleep at night?"

Not looking back Peri said, "With my eyes closed, Big Flower, with my eyes closed." He and William snickered, stifling louder laughter when a couple nurses glared at them in passing.

When Chrys reached the lobby of the main entrance to the hospital, she was surprised to see Jack sitting in one of the chairs. He got up when he saw her and walked toward her.

"How is she?" he asked.

"She's doing fine." She cocked her head. "What are you doing here?"

"I went to your house after I finished at Gram's and Peri told me what happened. So when your dad got there, I asked if I could ride along." He looked toward the elevators. "They wouldn't let me come up since I'm not family. How long's she gonna be here do you think?"

"The doctor said maybe Monday she could be released. That is, if she responds to the treatment."

"I guess that could put a kink in your plans."

"Plans?"

"The Uncle Jules thing."

Chrys looked down and shook her head. "That's all over. Peri and William are going to go on without Iris. And if they do that, then I'm out too."

"Then make them understand. Don't boss them, just make them see that it won't work unless all four of you are in." As she mulled over his words, he said, "Come on, you're Big Flower, aren't you?"

Chrys bristled at that nickname coming from his lips. But before she could voice her disapproval, the elevator doors opened and Peri and William stepped out, along with a candy-striper, the best-dressed girl in school who Chrys had seen walking to class with Jack a few times. As Chrys marched toward her brothers, the girl with dark hair and flawless skin sashayed past her, twinkling her made-up eyes at Jack and smiling coyly with glossy lips.

Chrys stopped her brothers and took them aside at an angle where she could keep her eye on Jack and that girl. Then she took an authoritative stance and said to her brothers, "Uncle Jules visited all of us. Obviously, he wanted

161

all of us to be part of this. So if you think you're going to find a treasure without Iris and me, you're wrong. And besides, you'll kill Iris—and you know it—if you go on without her."

While the boys seemed to chew on that, Chrys looked past Peri's shoulder and saw the dark-haired girl, laughing, lay her hand—bejeweled with pink fingernail polish—on Jack's chest. Chrys envisioned swatting the girl's hand then swatting the whole girl away like a fly. Before any other possibility played out in her mind, Peri spoke—or for the first time in Chrys's recollection, stuttered.

"Okay, I ... William and me ... well," he said as though he was studying the pattern in the commercial carpeting, "we promise to stand together as a four-some." Then before any sentimentality could enter the moment, he stood straight and said, "But I do have an idea." He peered intensely at Chrys. "With what you said upstairs we've got enough information to look up this story at the Willow Herald. Can I at least do that tomorrow, without Iris?"

Before answering, Chrys glanced over at Jack and the girl and saw Jack smiling and sauntering out the emergency doors with her. Chrys's mind could barely form an intelligible sentence. At last, she turned her back to Jack and the girl and recalling her interrogation of Mrs. Drymon, she told Peri, "Well ... I suppose *that* would be okay." She grinned as best she could at her brother for his understanding. "But only if I come with you."

As Peri and William walked past her toward the sitting area, she suddenly felt a presence at her back. She swung around and there was Jack inches from her. He raised his hand and yanked his thumb over his shoulder.

"Wrong girl," he said smiling, and he laced the fingers of his hand through hers.

CHAPTER 17

Chrys assumed that like most businesses, the newspaper would be open by nine a.m. Not knowing, though, how long it would stay open on Saturday, she suggested to Peri that they be out the door by eight-thirty. She didn't want to take any chance that they'd run out of time and have to come back Monday. Yes, she told Peri, they knew the month and year the incident happened, but she had no idea how long it would take them to go through every day's paper for perhaps several weeks, especially since the story might not have been front page news.

They rode into Willow at ten to nine. In fifteen or twenty minutes every parking spot would be filled and the sidewalks bustling with shoppers. But now the streets were still fairly empty. So they sailed on their bikes wherever they pleased and dodged around corners without much fear. The newspaper sat on the top of a hill a few blocks off the main drag, fairly remote from the stores and restaurants of downtown. It was one of the oldest buildings without major renovation in the town. Rumor had it that the owner, Malcolm Driscoll, thought the factory was haunted with the ghost of his grandfather so he refused to make any changes in the structure, other than repairs or painting, for fear that his grandfather's wrath would be visited upon him. But Chrys's mother had told her that Malcolm didn't have to worry about that. His grandfather had bestowed his "mark" on Malcolm decades before when he labeled him the black sheep of the family who would never amount to anything. So Malcolm and the newspaper never did amount to much. But, Chrys's mother said time and time again, as she paid the bill to keep the daily paper coming, that *The Herald* might not do much to address the many sides of national issues, but at least it did a respectable job of reporting local events. Chrys guessed that's why her family also received *The Cleveland Press*, *The Wall Street Journal*, and *The New York Times*.

The front of the building was old red brick from another century. Testifying to that were five gargoyles along the flat roof peering down at Chrys and Peri as they walked up the steps to the entrance. Peri reached out and grabbed the door handle. But before he could say anything, Chrys noticed the small sign in the window.

"They're closed," she said.

Peri yanked anyway. "Oh, great. What do we do now?"

After giving that a moment of thought, the perfect solution dawned on her. "The library."

"The library? I'm not standing around while you look for books to read."

"Not to check out books. To use their archives. I've seen people searching for stuff on microfilm. It just now occurred to me that some of them were scrolling through newspaper pages. But I don't know if they go back more than a decade."

Peri was down the steps and on his bike before Chrys got to that last sentence. She quickly jumped on her bike and managed to stay not far behind him as he wove through the now more congested city streets.

At the front desk of the library, they inquired how to go about finding an old article from *The Willow Herald*. The librarian indicated they'd find that in the reference section. As she held up her finger to point the way, Chrys said she knew where it was, thanked her and sped off, this time with

Peri at her heels.

A girl about Chrys's age was behind the counter. Chrys guessed she was one of the summer volunteers, what Chrys could have been if her mother hadn't insisted she find a job that paid by way of money instead of reading privileges. The girl was thin like Chrys and about the same height but she had the reddest hair Chrys had ever seen—naturally red and brighter than a new penny—and eyelashes so light in color they seemed to glow. The number of her freckles was quadruple those of Chrys's—so many, in fact, that in places they merged into patches that looked tanned. She wasn't unattractive, Chrys thought, just unfeminine. Uneasily, she thought she might be looking at a face similar to her own. So for the first time in her life, Chrys mentally played makeup artist with the girl's face and adorned it with mascara and a hint of light brown liner, then applied peach gloss to her lips. Much better, she thought. As Uncle Jules used to say, "Undeveloped potential amounts to nothing." Of course, he had said that about talent, but Chrys saw no reason why it couldn't apply to looks. She felt compelled to share this with the girl, but Chrys noticed her own worn jeans and baggy shirt and decided not to. When Chrys and Peri came up to the counter, the girl spoke right up and with the voice of a squawking parrot asked them if she could help. Sheesh, Chrys thought, that voice could use a visual distraction. And so she also painted onto the girl's face some gray-blue eye shadow. If she's going to sound like an annoying bird, then at least she should look like an exotic cat. The girl asked again what they needed and Chrys finally focused. She told the girl they were trying to find a newspaper article from May 1990. The girl swung around and walked over to a cabinet on the opposite wall. She pulled out a small box then motioned with her hand to follow her.

On an adjacent wall in the same reference section, the

girl pointed to one of two boxy-looking machines. Though it had a large screen for viewing, nothing else about the reading machine looked like a TV. The whole thing was white, including the screen, which was angled down a bit and recessed so that the top of the machine extended over it like an awning. Under the screen were knobs and a place to load the film. The girl asked if either of them knew how to operate it. When Chrys shook her head, the girl began rattling off a set of instructions so rapidly that Chrys stopped her mid-sentence and politely asked if she would load the film for them. The girl seemed delighted, and within a minute the machine was ready. Then slowly, as though the girl were speaking to a mentally handicapped person, she explained how to turn the knobs to advance the microfilm. Chrys would have said something snide—and poked Peri in the side when he opened his mouth—if their mission weren't so important. They needed to keep themselves in that girl's good graces should they need her assistance again.

Peri quickly advanced through the newpaper issues until he reached the third week of May. He slowed the pace so that they could examine every headline. Page by page went by of each local section, and day by day until they had searched through all two weeks' worth of papers. Nothing.

"It has to be here," Chrys said. "Go back to the beginning. We missed it."

"No we didn't," he said removing the film and rolling it up. Suddenly, his eyes lit up. "You know, I don't think school always ended in May like it does for us. I've heard older teachers talk about how school used to start after Labor Day."

Chrys grabbed the box from his hand, pulled out the film and rethreaded it. Peri again rolled through the first few months and then slowed down when he hit the first full week of June. Scrolling through the pages, they scrutinized the headlines. The week went by without a single headline of a death. Several minutes later and week two was finished with no mention of a girl's accident. But when Peri moved through the articles on Sunday, June 17, he suddenly blurted, "Oh my God, here it is!" so loudly that people sitting at nearby tables glared at him.

The headline read, "Girl's Climb Ends in Tragedy." The beginning paragraph of the article read, "Late Sunday afternoon, Allison Park, a twelve-year-old girl whose family recently moved to Willow, died after falling from a tree. The accident occurred on Schyul Road where the Park family was building a house. The girl fell from a tree house under construction and died en route to the hospital."

"Mom said their name was Peck."

"The paper wouldn't mistake a detail like that—not in a story about a girl's death." Then quietly he said, "That's it, don't you see?"

"What's it?"

"A park not a park."

"Oh my God, you're right." She pointed to the words "tree house." "And that's the other 'house not a house.'"

She stared at Peri as a shiver passed along her spine. "We missed it when we walked that property. I mean, I never thought to look up."

"Maybe it's not there anymore."

"It has to be."

Peri scratched his head. "What did Uncle Jules say to you that night, exactly?"

She closed her eyes for a second to see if Uncle Jules' exact wording would come to her. "'Everything you need is there. In the higher dwelling of the two ... but you must step very carefully.' Then he said it was "between two houses of great sadness." Peri, I think the treasure's buried somewhere in that backyard."

"Nah, you've got it wrong. He mentioned the two houses just so we'd find that particular piece of land. I'm betting the treasure's in that tree house." Rising he said, "And I say let's find out right now."

She grabbed his arm. "Monday. We've got to wait 'til Monday."

"Ahhh geez..."

"You promised to give Iris a chance to come. We're too close to finding the treasure to leave her out of this."

"Ahhh geez..."

"And no sneaking out there, either, with William."

"Ahhh geez, Big Flower, tie me up why don't you, and throw me into a closet for the rest of the weekend."

"Love to," Chrys said with smiling malice over his use of her nickname.

"Okay, okay. Let's get out of here," he said turning away.

"Hey, wait up," she said feeling that she'd been left holding the bag or rather, the microfilm. But he didn't look back or answer.

Not believing for a second he would wait for her, she sat for a minute longer and read the rest of the short article. It offered no more information that would help them find the treasure, but it did give her a richer understanding of how the girl's death must have affected the closeness of that family. By the father's quote that "It should never have happened," Chrys envisioned a man riddled with guilt over either wishing he hadn't built the tree house in the first place or wishing he had gotten it finished before Allison and Carrie, her older sister of sixteen, decided to climb up there. And Carrie would have also been agonized with self-loathing for permitting her sister to climb to the tree house without any walls or railing around it. And what about her thirteen-year-old twin brothers, who had left their metal bats beneath where she fell? Or her mother who saw them begin their climb and didn't see the danger in climbing just another tree? How easy it would have been, Chrys thought, for all the family members to point the finger of blame at themselves, or worse, at each other. And in no time, before they even realized what was happening, the fabric of their warm and loving family would be ripped to unmendable shreds.

Chrys removed the microfilm, placed it back in the box with respectful slowness as though laying Allison to rest, and turned off the machine. At the desk she presented the box to the red-haired girl who seemed astonished that Chrys had managed by herself and asked Chrys if there was anything else she could do for her. Chrys shook her head, said "Thanks anyway" and headed casually for the front doors. Presuming she'd be riding home with only her thoughts, she took a quick minute to check out the "New Additions" shelf. Finally stepping outside, she was surprised and gratified to see Peri waiting for her by the bike rack.

The hint of friendliness didn't last, however. When Peri sarcastically called her "Big Flower" again, she knew he had waited for her only to poke at her for stifling his suggestion to go out to "School Road." She responded by saying, "Too bad Mom wasn't growing pansies the summer she gave birth to you."

"What's that supposed to mean?"

"You can't climb a flight of stairs without getting dizzy."

Red-faced, he stuck his tongue out at her and sped off. Broiling too, she zoomed around a corner and caught sight of city hall. She contemplated stopping there to pick up the paperwork for changing her name and so glided her bike along the sidewalk closer and closer to it. But before reaching the building, she made a hairpin turn in the street, realizing that, like the Willow Herald, all government

169

buildings would be closed. Besides, she had to tackle the hard part first—getting her mother to say "yes" to the idea.

When she arrived home, her father suggested they go to the hospital to visit Iris, who was improving nicely, as well as relieve their mother who had spent the night there. Chrys and Peri were delighted with the chance to share the news with Iris. And as soon as Chrys and Peri filled William in, he also shared in the excitement of telling Iris and the relief of having something to do other than twiddle his thumbs or watch the hands of a clock inching with excruciating slowness. Chrys insisted that she be the one to trickle the information to Iris so she wouldn't freak out again. Peri wasn't speaking to Chrys so by way of William he communicated that he didn't see any reason for telling Iris anything. Chrys knew his suggestion might have been the safest way, but in Chrys's mind, it was the most dishonest one. If they were on this mission together, then Iris had a right to know, *should* know, as much as the rest of them. After all, hadn't she been the one who figured out Uncle Jules' clue to her?

As they entered Iris's room, she appeared as normal as could be, but their mother dashed Chrys's hope that Iris might be released before Monday. The IV would remain for at least another day and respiratory therapy for three or four more sessions. But hearing that the x-ray showed no congestion and Iris's blood gases were normalizing, Chrys crossed her fingers that her mother was wrong.

A half hour later, their parents left for the coffee shop and the boys took off for the gift store with twenty dollars their mother had given them, leaving Chrys alone with Iris. She debated about the rightness of Peri's statement, whether she should share the information right now or wait until Iris was definitely stable.

Suddenly, Iris said, "I've been thinking a lot about how

upset I got. And I've decided not to let anything else flip me out." She looked confidently at Chrys. "I'm not afraid anymore."

"Are you absolutely sure?"

Iris peered at her as though she was trying to read Chrys's mind. "Sure I'm sure. Why?"

Chrys rubbed her hands together. "Just wondered."

"What is it? You know something, don't you? I could sense it from Peri and William, too. The way they looked at each other."

Chrys shifted nervously in her seat. "Well, this morning Peri and I looked up a newspaper article about that girl's death." She took a deep breath. "Now get a grip, okay? Her last name was *Park* and she died by falling from a tree *house*."

Iris's eyes got large and she gave a little gasp.

"Are you all right?" Chrys asked, lurching forward. "Do you need the nurse?"

Iris shook her head and waved her off, then she whispered, "Only one more clue. 'A horn not a horn.'" She smiled broadly and quietly clapped her hands. "We're almost there." Still, her face grew stern. "But we've got to move fast."

Chrys got up and hugged her sister. "You *so* need to hold onto this attitude."

Their father walked in and smiled at the two of them. "I'm staying here for a couple hours while your mother and the boys go back to the house. You going too, Chrys?"

She glanced at Iris who gave her a thumbs up. "I guess," Chrys said. Then to Iris she said, "I'll be back for a long time—we'll play rummy or something. And then Monday, maybe—" And she held up crossed fingers of both hands. "—you'll be back home."

Their mother appeared in the doorway. She came over to Iris and kissed her, told her she'd be back later. The boys then entered with magazines and a puzzle book for her. They gave their well-wishes and left. Chrys walked out with their mother and put her arm around her waist.

"I'm glad Iris is coming around so fast," Chrys said.

Her mother wrapped her arm around Chrys's waist and sighed. "Me too. I think I'll actually be able to sleep tonight." She gave Chrys's waist a squeeze. "Getting back to normal feels so good."

"Hey, Mom?" Chrys asked tentatively.

"Yes?"

"About changing my name. I ... I really am sick of all the jokes I get."

Her mother's eyebrows rose in amazement. "I didn't know it was that bad or that it bothered you that much."

"Well it is and I am." She sucked in a breath and held it for a second. "You know, like Uncle Jules said, there's more than one way to die."

Her mother unhooked her arm from Chrys's waist and pushed the elevator button. Staring at the lit button, she said, "And when did Uncle Jules say that?"

Chrys knew her mother was questioning whether Chrys had learned that information before or after his death.

"It's the message in a short story he used to teach— 'Brother Death.'"

Her mother's shoulders began to quiver. "I guess I didn't realize…"

Chrys would have put her arm around her but she worried that her mother might burst into tears and forget that she understood how Chrys felt. Instead, she said softly, "It's not that I don't love my name and what it means; it's the spelling. Just one letter."

Her mother didn't exactly nod. Rather, she shook her head slightly as though inside it she was nudging a wooden block off the edge of a puzzle to make it fall into place. "Let me sleep on it, okay?" she said as the elevator opened.

That Saturday ground on like a millennium in hell. Peri remained a mute to Chrys, conveying what little he had to say through William, with William only too glad to play telegraph office. Between Peri's silence and Williiam's babbling on about how he couldn't wait to find the treasure, Chrys thought she would go stark raving mad. By Saturday evening she thought about calling Jack and seeing if they could hang out or merely pass some time on the phone about the new developments, but in calling his house, she got the answering machine. And when she tried his cell, it was turned off. She guessed he was out to dinner with his parents—they had a strict rule about using their phones in a restaurant. She left him a message to call her and staring at it, waited. When after several minutes the phone didn't ring, she waited some more. Then right on the verge of wanting to commit herself to an insane asylum, Old Navy called and asked her to start the following day, Sunday, noon to four. When she said she could, the manager read off the rest of her days and hours for that week. Monday, thank goodness, wasn't one of them.

When she got to the store, her supervisor said she would be refolding clothes and playing gopher to customers in the dressing rooms by bringing them garments she'd then re-hang or refold and put back where they belonged. As boring as the day was, she was still relieved to have had something to do. Plus, she loved the opportunity to get her hands on new shipments and try them on in the lulls between customers. Coming out of work, she clicked on her phone and noticed one missed call and a new text. It was Jack in both cases. He was sorry she couldn't reach him—dinner out with his parents the night before—and all day

Sunday a family reunion in southern Ohio with the same phone restriction. He'd call her late in the evening during the car ride back.

But that evening everyone seemed on edge, including Chrys, as though a full moon was moving the tide of their emotions. Their mother and father talked restlessly about whether Iris would come home the next day. Peri and William couldn't agree on a single activity to do together, even watch TV. Jack called at ten but by this time Chrys felt uneasy about repeating the story of the Park family and reliving the gloominess that had haunted her after reading the article. So she limited their talk to his family reunion and her first day at work, then abruptly said she'd have to go. When he warily asked why, she adopted a soothing voice and said it wasn't him. She was simply exhausted. He understood, wished her "pleasant dreams" and told her to call him the following day when she was feeling better.

After hanging up, Chrys stared at the framed Shakespearean quote from Uncle Jules in her room and, like her mother, obsessed about how things had been better when he was alive. A part of her—she couldn't tell if it was that previous imp upon her shoulder—said finding the treasure would make all things right. Another part—another little creature now sitting on her other shoulder and whispering in her ear—said it couldn't possibly. But whether she and the others failed or succeeded in finding the treasure—one way or the other—Chrys knew things would never be the same.

CHAPTER 18

At eleven on Monday, Chrys stood nervously at the kitchen window as her mother pulled the car to the back of the house but stopped in front of the closed garage door. Iris was finally home. Given the nail-biting wait over the weekend, Chrys thought a fanfare of streamers and trumpets would have been a fitting welcome. Instead, Iris seemed just as pleased to see Chrys flailing her arms on the back stoop and hear the boys hooting in falsetto.

Their mother, who had taken off half a day to pick her up, left the car running as she followed Iris inside. Pointing at each of the four, she repeated the doctor's discharge orders. Before anyone could turn away or take a breath, she repeated them again to make sure everyone understood how "imperative it was to follow the instructions to a 'T,' if not to a UVWXY and Z." Chrys appreciated the humor in that; her mother was once again slipping in some levity in order to get them to do as she wanted. Chrys had always admired her mother for understanding how hard it was for kids to take an ultimatum when it sounded too much like one. Still, her mother emphasized that over the next few days—to prevent a relapse—Iris was to experience "no sustained or strenuous activity and no emotional agitation." Then she handed Chrys the bag of new medications, a new nebulizer medicine and a timed release inhaler that only a parent would administer twice a day. Then she bear-hugged Iris much longer than usual and told Iris she'd see her in only a few hours.

As soon as she drove away, Iris folded her hands in front of her and said, "Well, I'm ready."

"Ready for what?" Peri asked.

"For going out to 'School' Road and finding the treasure, silly."

Chrys quickly stepped in. "Did they do something at the hospital to make you deaf? Did you not hear what Mom said—twice?"

"But we've got to move fast. I told you that," Iris said picking up her hospital bag and walking toward the kitchen door. Before leaving, she turned around. "When we passed the property, there was a big piece of machinery parked on it."

"What kind of machinery?" William asked.

"I don't know. But it had a big shovel on one end."

"A pay loader," Peri said. "I'll bet somebody will be out there tomorrow on it—at daybreak."

"Now *you're* having visions?" Chrys asked.

"Not me," he said pointing at himself. "I just know that those machines cost a lot of money. They don't let them sit forever before using them."

Iris said from the doorway, "I'm ready when you guys are."

"No," Chrys said. "No. No. No. If we ride out there again and anything happens to Iris, we'll all be dead or want to be. It's not just the punishment we've got to think about ... it's Iris."

Iris walked over to her. "I know I can do it. If I'm not afraid any more, then nothing's going to happen."

"Well, maybe that's taken care of, and maybe it isn't, but there's still the ride out there. And that's a chance we can't take and an order we can't break." She thought of her appointment at noon with Dr. Belmont, a second rule that would be broken.

"I know!" William blurted. "We'll carry her! If her asthma is the only thing stopping us, then we'll each take turns."

Peri's eyes gleamed. "Perfect, my man." And he patted William's back.

Chrys looked suspiciously at all of them for a minute. Could they really pull it off by "carrying" Iris out there? Would she really not freak out with what she knew about the girl's death? Chrys again heard comments from those creatures sitting on her shoulder, only now both simultaneously drummed into her ears. A mixture of passionate urges to go onward and stern warnings to stay home filled her ears and crashed together in her brain like two stags bashing foreheads. They were so close to completing their mission but their mother had put a stop to it. And for good reason: Iris. She was worth the sacrifice, Chrys thought. Never again did Chrys want to see her in the state she was in Friday night. No, the price was way too high.

"I ... I can't do it," Chrys said, "treasure or no treasure. Uncle Jules will just have to understand." She took a step back and crossed her arms.

Iris, frail little Iris, seemed to grow an inch taller. Her face radiated a glow Chrys had never seen on her sister's pale skin. And Iris's eyes widened with purpose. "Please," with a beggar's voice she said. "Please let's do this. It's what Uncle Jules wants."

All six eyes turned to Chrys. She realized that what she said would change the course of all of them. What she would say, either way, would decide an outcome for all of them that none of them could imagine. If she could guarantee Iris's protection against another asthma attack in getting her out there and if Iris could guarantee that she would withstand the emotional impact of searching for the treasure, then how could she refuse? No rule would be broken, no harm done.

177

And as William had said earlier, would Uncle Jules have put them on a path they couldn't travel to its end? Surely, he would have intervened and closed the door on this himself if it wasn't meant to be. If he could start this mission, certainly he could end it too.

"Okay," Chrys said as though swallowing her tongue in the process. "But *all* our heads will roll if we aren't careful."

"I like that," Peri said winking.

"You like what?" Chrys said.

"That Shakespeare talk."

Chrys made a face at him to shut him up and grabbed Iris by the shoulders. Before she could speak, though, Iris said, "I won't let any of you down." As that remark settled in, Iris glanced at the clock on the stove. "Can we please go now before this *waiting* gives me an attack?"

While Iris took her bag upstairs, Peri, William and Chrys buzzed about the kitchen, packing up drinks and snacks and this time, chocolate bars for a hopeful celebration. Iris appeared a few minutes later brandishing her emergency inhaler and off they shot through the back door.

The mileage to the property seemed twice as long this time since Iris's weight slowed down any of them, even Peri. And going up the steeper hills meant for all of them to dismount and walk the incline. Once, Chrys looked over and imagined seeing Cleopatra being carried by bearers whose arms rippled with the weight of her carriage. Well, at least they didn't have to literally carry Iris or fan her either. But she acted far from the queen. She willingly offered to walk when the way became difficult, but Chrys assured her that when the road got hard was especially the time when Iris should be Cleopatra perched on her cushions.

By the time they descended that last hill and saw the edge of the property, Chrys thought only a Samurai's sword could have cut the tension in the air. Sneakily, she glanced at

Iris to assess her emotional strength. To Chrys's surprise her eyes were calm, her brow smooth, and her lips turned up at the corners as though she was posing for a wistful photograph with a new-born puppy. Then Chrys stared across the property and caught a glint of dark yellow. Within a few more seconds the pay loader came into full view. Thank goodness it was still just sitting there and in the same spot Iris had said it was. And no cars or other vehicles were parked along the dirt road. Everyone seemed to see and understand that they had made the right decision, for the four sighed deeply. As though their voices would break the magic of the moment, they, instead, exchanged looks and nods as agreement to embark upon that plot of earth.

Before they got too far, Chrys stopped them and asked Iris if she felt she could walk the depth of the property or whether she and Peri should put their hands together and carry her the rest of the way. Iris giggled and said, "No more Cleopatra for me." So onward they walked, Chrys fixing her eyes on where the basement would appear, Peri peering beyond it to the trees in the back.

A minute later, standing on the back edge of the basement, Chrys said, "Iris, you stay here. The three of us will scout those trees. Peri you take the one on the left. William, straight ahead. I'll take the one to the right of us."

They fanned out and each approached the huge maple trees with leaves so broad and abundant that not seeing a tree house in any of them would be purely understandable. Chrys saw peripherally and occasionally turned to see that Peri and William reached their trees first and slowly walked around them peering intently into its branches. They cocked their heads this way and that and even stepped close and pressed their bodies against the trunk to make sure they hadn't missed anything. At last, each called out that they saw nothing peculiar. By this time Chrys was under her tree and circling it as the boys had done. A third of the way around, her heart started beating so wildly she could barely call out.

Beginning in a whisper and growing louder each time she said, "Come here, come here, come here!" Peri and William sprinted toward her. She quickly spun around to Iris.

While the boys clambered over and Iris strained like a dog on an imaginary leash, Chrys stared up, walking from side to side to see it from all angles. Then stepping backward, her right foot slipped on an exposed root and her ankle crunched sideways. She screamed in pain and dropped to the ground. Peri and William and now Iris rushed over.

Grabbing her arm, Peri said, "Can you stand on it?"

Still wincing, Chrys allowed him to help her up. She tested her footing. "I think it will be okay to bike, but looking up she said, "I don't trust it to climb this tree."

The others now following her gaze gasped in seeing a small wooded floor built ten or twelve feet in the air between three great boughs. The wood had weathered over all those years into the same color as the bark. And in a couple places green and sky showed through large knotholes.

Peri's head lowered first. "You can't climb? Then who—?" He looked around to see William and Iris staring at him. He took a nervous breath and looked back at Chrys.

She gave him a thumbs up, then patted him on the back. "Perfect, my man!" With shallow worry lines deepening into trenches, he shifted his weight from one foot to the other. He shoved his hands in his pockets and pawed at the ground.

"Come on, Peri," Chrys said. "Just take it one step at a time." She encouraged him with pats on the back. "I'll climb you through it."

He glared up at the tree as though he wished he had brought a chain saw. Chrys gave him a slight nudge and pointed to the pay loader. She grabbed his arm and hobbled a few feet around the trunk. Above the bottom, low-hanging bough she pointed to boards nailed in the trunk as evenly spaced as rungs on a ladder.

"Piece of cake," she said.

William stammered, "Maybe I should do this—and be the one to find the treasure. I can climb this ol' tree." He clutched the branch and lifted his leg over it.

Peri grabbed William's arms and brought them down. "No. I'm the one who believed the treasure was up there, so I'm going to be the one who finds it."

As soon as William had both feet on the ground, Peri started his ascent. Chrys noticed how shaky he was in taking hold and stepping up but she cautioned him not to look down and to listen carefully to everything she told him to do. Peri obviously hadn't seen that the top board was missing and he'd have to do a bit of branch climbing to reach the platform.

Slowly, hand over hand he moved along like a squirrel in slow motion. Sweat beaded up on his forehead and several times he wiped one hand then the other on his shirtfront. Upward he went chewing or licking his lips and sometimes sticking out the tip of his tongue like first graders hoping to write a perfect alphabet. At last, he reached the missing last step.

Without looking down, he yelled, "There's no more steps! Didn't you see that? What am I going to do now?" Before any of them could respond, he reached down with his foot and said, "I know what I'm going to do. I'm coming down!"

"Peri! Wait!" Chrys called out sharply. "You're only a few feet away. It's easy I tell you. It's really easy. Just do what I say."

Still without looking down he paused, then finally nodded.

"Okay, there's a medium sized branch to your left that you should be able to get your arms around and then you're going to walk your legs up the trunk to it and wrap them around the limb too so you're hanging upside down. You scoot along the branch until it intersects with the big one the tree house is built on and then you'll be able to right yourself and crawl along it on your hands and knees to get onto the platform."

This time he jerked his head down a little to see her out of one eye. "Are you out of your flippin' mind? I'm no rubber-jointed marsupial with a tail for a hand, you know!"

Chrys chuckled.

"This isn't funny."

"No but 'marsupial' was. And picturing you with a tail," she said under her breath. Yelling up she told him, "I had no idea your intellect was so far-reaching."

"Well, it sounded better than 'chimpanzee.'" Chrys saw his shoulders shake and then he burst into a gale of nervous laughter. "Yeah, where's Cheetah or Ling Ling when you need a tree jockey?"

A long pause followed. Chrys thought he might be giving himself an internal pep talk or even praying. None of them on the ground broke the silence. Then Peri nodded his head a couple times as though going over the tactical maneuvers a final time, plotting which hand to move first, which foot first to ensure the greatest success. Finally, his left arm reached out and encircled the limb. The other followed and then his feet. He took a deep breath and stretched out his arms a little way and slid his legs along. Like an inverted caterpillar he inched along until he reached the large bough. With the help of a small branch near his hands he twisted his body up and around until he lay on top of the large limb. He was huffing by this time and Chrys hoped he wouldn't get dizzy. She got him to stop for a moment to relax.

Calmer a minute later, he crawled on and reached the platform safely. As though venturing onto thin ice, he crept over it, testing each board to make certain it was sturdy enough to hold his weight. About halfway across what appeared to be a five or six foot expanse, he disappeared completely from view.

After a few seconds of silence, Chrys called up, "Peri, you okay?"

She heard a sliding sound from above. Peri's head popped up and then they could see him scooting toward them on his bottom to the edge of the platform where he sat with his legs dangling over the side, a paper clutched in his hand.

"What did you find?" William bellowed excitedly.

"Not the treasure," Peri said reluctantly while staring down at Chrys.

"It's okay," she said without a twinge of smugness. "Show us what you did find."

He dropped the paper and started his descent. "It was sealed in a Christmas tin."

Chrys motioned to the twins not to touch it. To Peri, knowing he was facing the hard part, she said, "You need help?"

He smiled with confidence. "I ... I think I can handle it."

Still, Chrys watched him anyway. She thought about suggesting another route as there was an offshoot he could take which swooped close enough to the ground so he could hang from it and then drop the last three feet instead, but she decided what he'd accomplished already was enough therapy for the day.

When he landed at the bottom, his face looked as though he wanted to kneel down and kiss the ground. Instead, he dusted himself off and walked over proudly.

Chrys picked up the paper and carefully unfolded it.

"Look northwest from the edge and you'll see it," the note said.

Chrys thought back to her conflict with Peri about where the treasure would be. "I think it means from the front edge of the basement."

She tromped away to find out and the others followed. For some time they searched with tiny steps or got on their knees when they came to patches of grass too tall to see the earth through it. Finally, Chrys admitted she must have been mistaken.

"But what else could it have meant?" William asked.

"The tree house," Iris piped up. "The edge of the tree house."

Peri's face grew red. "I'm not going up there again!" He looked at their faces. "No, I've had enough communing with that tree for one day."

"You've got to, Peri," Chrys said.

"Naw, let William go up there this time."

"Well, why didn't you read the note while you were up there," Chrys barked. "That would have saved us all a lot of aggravation."

"I was only trying to be considerate." He got in her face. "I mean, you're the one constantly talking about doing all this together."

For several minutes they bickered until both threatened to pack it up and go home. When they actually turned and started to walk away, Iris began to cry softly like a wounded animal. William ran up to them.

"You can't just leave. Look at Iris. Is that what you two want? Iris back in the hospital?"

Chrys looked at Peri questioningly. Peri, sighed, put his hands on his hips and nodded. The ax was buried.

"But who's going up there?" Peri asked pointing.

"Cause it's not going to be me."

As if William's face were a light bulb, it lit up brightly. "Maybe no one has to. Uncle Jules said it has to do with these two houses and if we draw a straight line northwest from the tree house, wouldn't the corner of the basement land along it—maybe?"

"Maybe," Peri said rubbing his chin. "And maybe we don't have to be quite as high as the platform to see what we're supposed to. Come on, I have an idea."

Back at the tree Peri positioned himself directly under the tree house and faced the southeast corner of the basement. He instructed William to get on his shoulders, grab the branch above him and stand up. William did as he was told. From that height he peered out along the invisible line he drew with his mind. And just about the time he was ready to give up, clouds above opened up and the sun illuminated every green blade and bald spot on that property.

William's wide eyes glinted even in the shade of that big tree. "There's something bright up ahead. Like sun on metal."

Chrys recalled her early trip to the halfway house and how a wad of foil had looked the same way. "Are you sure you see something? Maybe it's just the reflection off a rock."

"No, I can actually see a couple things shining."

He jumped down and they all followed him to the spot. Chrys wondered how he was so sure to be accurate, but he had always been good at visually marking the lie of a golf ball as it landed. When he stopped, Chrys noticed they were halfway between the basement and the tree house and realized her uncle's comment about being "between two houses of sadness" might have been literal. She looked down and saw not two but four glints in the grass. The clouds covered up the sun again and the objects went dull. So that's why they hadn't seen them the day they walked the property!

185

William got down on his knees and spread the grass with his fingers. The others followed.

"What are they?" Iris asked of the four pieces of metal imbedded in the shape of a circle.

William dug in his fingers and pulled one out while Chrys questioned whether he should.

He held it up. They all looked dumbfounded.

"It's a shoe horn!" William yelled. "A horn not a horn!"

"How do you know what that is?" Chrys asked.

"I saw Dad use one once in a store when he was trying on dress shoes, only that one was plastic with a long handle."

"So let's dig in everybody," Peri suggested. "They look like shovels to me. Uncle Jules thought of everything—there's one for each of us." He paused and looked up at the tree house.

"What?" Chrys asked.

"It's funny. Some of the nails were as rusted as could be and others looked brand new." He looked back at her and she nodded at him.

Feverishly, the four burrowed into the circle of earth. Peri flung scoops of dirt over his shoulders; Chrys and Iris placed the clods between them in a common pile and William cast his between his straddled legs as a dog does when excavating a bone.

It was Peri who first hit something hard. Then Iris. He motioned the others back to dig the rest by hand. What he lifted from the foot-deep hole was a padded yellow box wrapped in clear plastic. Chrys informed everyone that it looked similar to Aunt Lydia's jewelry box and Iris agreed. They allowed Peri to undo the plastic, though Chrys's heart was pounding out of her chest. She looked over at Iris who hugged Chrys with anticipation. Chrys, whispering, asked Iris whether they should stop. Iris shook her head.

The plastic off, Peri released the latch and lifted the lid.

Music immediately filled their ears. A dancer on a lake of mirror spun in a continuous pirouette.

"It *is* Aunt Lydia's jewelry box," Chrys said. "It plays the same music with the same purple velvet inside. I saw it on her pile to give to Goodwill."

"Open the black box. Open it!" William said pointing.

Chrys picked up the gift box and creaked open the lid. One ring with four differently colored stones stood up in the slot.

"Ooooh," Iris said.

The boys' hands swooped over to touch it but Chrys pushed them all away. "We've got to read the note first."

She could see through the paper that it was written in her uncle's calligraphy. She opened it slowly for fear of tearing it and read it out loud. "Chrys, Peri, William and Iris, you are finally where your mother and I always wanted you to be, growing side by side in the same sunny garden. That's the real treasure. You never realized you possessed it all along. Now maybe you'll never forget it. But if you should ever happen to, these rings will remind you. My love eternally, Uncle Jules."

"What rings?" William said with glassy eyes.

"These," Chrys said and she pulled out the "ring" from the box and separated them into four, each sporting its own gem. "They're engraved inside with our flower names. This one with the yellow topaz is mine. Here, Peri, the blue sapphire is yours. The purple amethyst goes to Iris and the rose garnet is William's.

"Ah, gee," William said, "did I have to get the pink one?"

"They're the colors of the flowers we were named after." Chrys said and smiled. "William, think light red instead."

Chrys slipped hers on her ring finger. Iris did the same.

The boys found their rings fit on their pinkies. William reached over and took the note from her hand and reread it.

"I wish he wasn't gone," he said and tears spilled down his cheek.

Chrys looked up to see Iris crying so hard she was shaking and Peri wiping tears away as fast as they came.

"Oh, but he's not," Chrys said holding up her hand with the ring on it. "Come, give me your hand, William. You too, Peri. And give Iris the other. Iris, you take William's." All of them complied. "See, we're a circle just like the rings Uncle Jules gave us. As long as we're connected he'll be standing right there in the center."

They lifted their clasped hands and with all eyes wet with tears, they nodded in silent acknowledgement of that fact. Finally, after seconds of silence and hard swallowing, they broke the chain. William bent down and picked up the jewelry box, opened it and peered at the dancer. Seeing a tab, he pulled on it.

"Hey, there's another compartment underneath!" He slid out the tray "And another note!"

The others came close as he opened it. The top of the paper was filled with random fireflies each drawn with a line of dashes trailing behind it to show its flight pattern.

"Fireflies?" Peri said.

"Fireflies, yes," Chrys said. Then she screamed, "Hey, I get it! Of course, it all makes sense now!"

"What does?" they all said.

"His explanation of why fireflies don't stay lit. Don't you remember?"

"Yeah, kinda," Peri said. "Something about not being able to fly by their own light...."

"Only by the light of the others," Iris finished.

"Exactly," Chrys said.

"Huh?" William said.

"Don't you see? It's what he made the four of us do."

Iris suddenly looked down and ominously said, "Uh oh."

Worried, Chrys put her hand on Iris's shoulder. "What is it? Do you need some help?"

"We're all going to need some," Iris said and grinned broadly. "Uncle Jules has done it to us again. Look." She pointed to the bottom of the page where in small print it started, "Look for a fish that's not a fish...."

"Yahoo!" yelled William, jumping up and down and waving an imaginary cowboy hat.

The other three looked with amazement at each other, laughed hysterically and then waving their invisible Stetsons, they shouted to the heavens, "Yahoo—ey!

CHAPTER 19

Regardless of Chrys's sore ankle or Iris's asthma, no one seemed to notice this time how long it took them to get home. Every step was a celebration and a reason for a bite from a Hershey's Special Dark Chocolate bar. They were happy, proud, and for the first time, each other's friend. Sitting on the railing of the interstate overpass, they made a pact about it. They touched rings as though they had pricked their fingers and were mingling their blood, vowing they would never again say anything mean-spirited to each other. "Mind you," Peri asked, before touching his ring to the others', "this doesn't mean we can't ever have an honest-to-goodness argument, does it?" When the other three nodded, he obliged, and so the seal, Chrys felt sure, was set in all their minds and hearts.

Pulling into the driveway later, Chrys saw their mother's car in the garage. She looked at the others who were staring with gaping mouths.

"What'll we do?" Peri said.

"We'll play it by ear," Chrys said. "Let me do the talking."

No one opposed.

When they went in, the house was deadly quiet. No sound—not a TV or radio or computer screen—spoke out. Beyond the kitchen they tiptoed through the house. At the stairs there was still no sign of their mother but a rustle of papers came from the den. Peri, William and Iris slunk upstairs. Chrys peeked around the open door. Her mother, wearing her reading glasses, was sitting at the desk doing paperwork. Chrys shuffled backward and brushed against the silk plant at the base of the stairs.

"Chrys, if that's you, would you come here, please."

Chrys walked over and stood in the doorway. "Hey," Chrys said. "What are you doing home? I thought you just took the morning off."

Her mother removed her glasses and turned in her chair. "I got worried about Iris, especially when no one answered the phone. Where have all of you been? I tried your cell phone too."

Chrys felt her pants pocket. "Oh, I guess I left it in my room. Sorry."

"And Dr. Belmont's office called me to say you canceled the appointment. So where did all of you go with Iris?"

Chrys came over and dragged her mother from the chair and onto the sofa next to her.

"This is bad, isn't it?" her mother said. "Just come out with it, Chrys," she said cupping her head in her hands.

"Not really. It depends on how you look at it."

Her mother looked askance at her from between her fingers. "Yes, it does depend on how I look at it."

"Okay, here goes. We went back to 'School' Road." Her mother's great intake of air didn't deter her, though. "But Iris didn't ride out there, honest."

"She wasn't with you?"

"Well, she was but—"

"But what? The Jetta was still sitting in the garage."

"We carried her out there piggyback on our bikes. We took turns. I promise you, she's absolutely fine. She didn't exert a single muscle or have a single panic button pushed."

Her mother sat up, leaned against the back of the couch

191

and laid her hands in her lap. "Why would all of you do such a thing? What could be so important about that place?"

Out of her back pocket Chrys produced Uncle Jules' first letter from the jewelry box. Her mother read and cried and said she didn't understand. Chrys reminded her of Uncle Jules' visitation, the quest he had put them on, and then the extent of their journey to solve the mystery.

At the end of her story, her mother said wiping her eyes, "I'm sorry. I didn't believe you." She picked up Chrys's hand and ran her fingers over the ring. "But hearing what you've said, seeing this and knowing how Julius was, I do now." She held Chrys to her.

Tears that had neatly pooled in Chrys's eyes now cascaded down her face. Try as she might to halt them, new ones raced behind them, hot and stinging, and her face grew wetter and wetter. Her eyes squeezed tight and she sobbed over the memory of Uncle Jules until her quaking shoulders and lungs were exhausted.

After a long pause in which she worked at catching her breath, Chrys said, "I feel it now."

"Feel what?"

"The emptiness."

Her mother smiled. "But you've been telling me all along that he's still with us. And he is, just in a different way than you meant. We carry him with us. Whether it's his sense of humor. His pranks. His warmth. His wisdom. All of these and more. As long as we live, he does too."

Chrys nodded and smiled. After more silence she asked, "So Mom, about our going out there ... are we going to be punished?"

Her mother bit her lip. "Well ... you did use good judgment in keeping Iris from another attack. And I never said she couldn't leave the house." She put Chrys at arms-length. "So I guess you're all off the hook."

Chrys smiled and slid to the edge of the sofa but before getting up she said, "Mom, one more thing that's been bugging me. You were usually in on Uncle Jules' jokes. Were you in on this one, too?"

Her mother, sniffling with a tissue to her nose, said, "No, Sweetie." She looked Chrys in the eye and took a breath. "Because this was no joke."

Chrys nodded and started to get up. Her mother stopped her by stroking her back. She seemed to run her fingers over her back, not as though she was trying to work out a knot in Chrys's muscles but one in her own mind. Finally, she stopped and said, "Chrys ... you can change your name if you want to."

Chrys swiveled around, gently kissed her on the cheek, and hugged her with all her might. "Thanks," she said with more heart than she had ever said that word, "but I think I'd like to keep it."

Her mother looked amazed.

"Oh, yes," Chrys said getting up, "I plan on naming all my children after flowers—nasturtium, hyacinth, caladium, phlox—all boys."

Her mother laughed and then Chrys matched her in barreling volume and intensity. As they were reduced to giggles moments later, the doorbell rang. Chrys excused herself and answered it by cracking the door.

It was Jack.

Without opening the door farther, she said, "Hi. I'll be right out."

She quickly closed the door and raced upstairs. A few minutes later she breezed back down with eyelashes a shade darker than her hair and wearing the same outfit she had seen in the window at Old Navy—but with standard black flip-flops. In the dip of her collarbone lay that Tiffany heart pendant her uncle had given her. When she opened the door, Jack grabbed her hand and pulled her outside.

He let her go and took a step back to look at her. "Hey, wow. You look great. So you ditched the jeans and polos...."

"Not all of them. They have their place. Sometimes."

"Good. I like you in them, too." He stepped close to her. "I tried reaching you all day. So tell me. What happened? Did you find it?"

"Uh huh," she said holding up her hand and twisting off the ring. "*We're* the treasure, see?" She pointed to her flower-name inscribed inside the band. "Isn't it wonderful?"

"I ... I'm not sure I understand."

She stooped down and picked two chrysanthemums from her mother's garden. She placed one behind his ear and the other in her ponytail. After slipping the ring on her finger again, she kissed him on the cheek and whispered, "Oh, I've got so much to tell you about today." Her voice electrified. "And there's another mystery...." She took a few steps toward the house to retrieve the note.

Jack caught up with her and grabbed her arm. "Not before solving this one," he said, and after pulling her close to him, pressed his lips to hers.